"I want to be married at Christmas.

"We should know by then whether or not it'll work." Adam's tone was matter-of-fact, but his eyes were hopeful.

"Christmas," Marissa said, then slowly nodded. "Okay, deal." She stuck out her hand.

"Deal," he repeated, ignoring her offer of a handshake. Instead he lowered his head and kissed her deeply.

Passion flared and burned brightly within her, and as Adam pulled her closer Marissa realized he was as excited as she. When at last he broke the kiss, resting his forehead against hers, she asked breathlessly, "Do you always seal a deal like that?"

"This is a first," he admitted hoarsely. "Do you suppose we should work out a few more details?"

A smile tugged at the corners of her mouth. "Absolutely. And I know just the place for such delicate negotiations...."

Rita Clay Estrada was once quoted as saying, "While I don't believe that love makes the world go around, I firmly believe that it's the magic ingredient that makes it all worthwhile." This philosophy shines through in *A Little Magic*, yet another wonderfully satisfying love story by this talented and dedicated romance writer.

Rita manages a busy life in Houston, Texas, dividing her time between her books and her family.

Books by Rita Clay Estrada

HARLEQUIN TEMPTATION

48–THE WILL AND THE WAY
72–A WOMAN'S CHOICE
100–SOMETHING TO TREASURE
136–THE BEST THINGS IN LIFE
166–THE IVORY KEY

A Little Magic

RITA CLAY ESTRADA

Harlequin Books

TORONTO • NEW YORK • LONDON
AMSTERDAM • PARIS • SYDNEY • HAMBURG
STOCKHOLM • ATHENS • TOKYO • MILAN

For three very special someones:
Marissa Allen, Little Mother;
Rebecca Holt, Artist;
and Rita Lou Estrada, Earth Science Teacher.
My golden girls . . .

Published January 1988

ISBN 0-373-25288-9

Printed in Canada

1

MARISSA MADISON stared into her coffee cup as if it were a crystal ball holding the answers she so desperately needed. She ignored the constant stream of people marching by the small café in the middle of one of the largest shopping malls in the country. Occasionally she searched the sea of humanity for Adam Pierce, then swiftly glanced down at her cup again. She was afraid to see him, and, conversely, she was afraid he wouldn't show up.

Words formed sentences in her head as she rehearsed what she would say to him. *Remember the alumni party last April when you finally noticed me and took me to bed? Well, guess what?*

No.

Remember the fun we had at the alumni party three months ago? Well, now it's time to pay the bill. Literally.

No.

An attractive older woman talking to her teenage daughter walked by, and Marissa's heart constricted. Her mother. How was she going to tell her mother and face the disappointment in her eyes? Having grown up in a fatherless family, Marissa should have known how hard it was for a woman alone to raise a child—as her mother had done.

And her stepfather? How could she explain that despite all the dire warnings issued and the living examples of her own parents she'd had to learn from, she still had screwed up. Royally. For one fleeting moment she had naively thought she'd be exempt from the dangers others were subject to—after all, she'd been in love and it had been only once. They were going to be so hurt....

Panic filled her again, just as it had off and on for the past month and a half. Scrabbling her hand on the floor, she reached for her purse. She couldn't go through with this. She had to get out of here, go hide somewhere. Find another solution.

Tears pressed against her eyelids and she valiantly held them at bay. This wasn't the time. When she reached her apartment, then she would allow herself to cry.

"Hello, Marissa."

Purse strap finally in her hand, she raised her head slowly and stared at Adam. He was smiling, and his smile broke her heart. She had wanted and waited for that smile for three years. And now it was going to be sheer torture to watch it disappear—to be replaced with anger that would tear her insides apart; anger that, she knew, would remain for a long time. "Hello, Adam."

Dressed in a dark gray, three-piece suit, he was as imposing as he was handsome. He slipped into the chair across from her, and she marveled at his grace. The man was both good-looking and rich. What a lethal combination—and one that would make it almost impossible for him to believe that what she had to say was not a trap in disguise.

She followed the movement of his dark head as he turned and motioned to the waitress for a cup of coffee for himself and a refill for her. His gray eyes were invisible, covered by brass-framed glasses that were light sensitive and slightly shaded to eliminate the glare of the hot Houston sun and the fluorescent brightness of the mall.

When he turned back he caught her staring, and he smiled again, but this time there was the hint of a question there. Marissa lowered her head, praying she could dredge up enough nerve to go through with this. What choice did she have?

"Your call sounded urgent. What's up?"

"Have you seen Elizabeth lately?" she asked, stalling for time. Elizabeth had been Adam's live-in for the past three years. They had broken up just before the alumni party.

The waitress set a cup of coffee in front of Adam and gave him a more than cursory once-over, obviously liking what she saw. Marissa commiserated.

"Last week. Why?" His tone was guarded as he removed his glasses and set them carefully on the table.

"Just wondered."

Adam slowly turned the cup in its saucer as he studied her, and she prayed her makeup hid the ravages of crying. The ravages of worrying. The ravages of trying to find answers where none existed. "If you wanted to invite me out, Marissa, all you had to do was come by the restaurant or call my office. What's this all about?"

His restaurant. His office. His apartments. His ground. No, this was better. This was more public and he wouldn't cause a scene because there were people everywhere they turned. Without conscious thought, she tilted her chin in the air. "I'm pregnant, Adam."

His hand stopped turning the cup. Not a muscle twitched. Her heart dropped to her toes as she watched the warmth in his eyes ebb to be replaced by a look of blue-gray steel. Her hands were shaking so hard she placed them in her lap so he wouldn't see.

"How far along?"

She swallowed hard. "Three months."

"Are you sure?"

She nodded, her eyes dropping away from his. She couldn't stand the rejection, the lack of emotion from him. It hadn't been all her fault. It took two people to make a relationship, even a one-night-stand kind of relationship. She lifted her head. "I'm sure. The doctor confirmed it a month ago."

His eyes narrowed. "Why are you telling me?" he asked softly, and she accepted the question as the challenge it was.

"Because you're the father."

"Who says?"

"I do."

He raised a dark brow. "What proof do you have?"

Her eyes bored into his with shining honesty. "My word, Adam. If you like, we can go through the tests to prove it, but you'll have to wait until the baby's born. I understand they're ninety-nine percent accurate now.

There hasn't been anybody else before or since you." Her soft voice was filled with conviction.

His look sliced through her. "Before?" he drawled in ridicule. "You weren't a virgin, Marissa."

"No," she repeated softly. "I wasn't a virgin. But there hasn't been anyone since college, Adam."

"Four years?" His look was disbelieving. "My, my, aren't we the innocent one." His sarcastic tone dragged along her spine, setting nerve endings on edge. She should have known he would react this way. After all, she'd had over a month to adjust to the news, he'd just learned of it two minutes ago. Who was she kidding? Even with a month's notice, she hadn't adjusted to it!

She took a slow, deep breath. "I know this is a shock to you. It's a shock to me, too. We both know how babies are made, and yet we fell into the oldest trap in the world: sex, pure and simple."

He stared at her. "And now you expect me to pay for this the rest of my life, right?"

"No," she denied quickly, shaking her head from side to side. "I'm asking for help with the next six months, the hospital and the doctor bills and the first six months after the baby is born. After that, I'll never bother you again. I promise."

He leaned forward, an errant wave of dark hair drifting down on his forehead. His eyes narrowed, delving into hers, spiking her with shards of guilt in places she was already wounded. "How do I know that you'll keep your end of the bargain? Because you say so?"

"I'll sign a contract. In fact, I'd rather do it that way. All I'm asking for is some financial help, not your life and limbs."

"Why not get an abortion?" He leaned back, relaxing as his narrowed gaze continued to inspect her.

She dropped her eyes and gave a choked laugh. "Believe me, I thought of it. A lot. But I'm having the baby instead."

"Adoption?"

She shook her head. "I don't think so. Lots of unwed mothers are keeping their babies today." She wished her voice didn't sound so tight and high, rasping with tension that couldn't be disguised.

"Are they schoolteachers, too?" he asked dryly, and she flinched. At least he remembered her occupation.

Her chin lifted. "It's my problem, I'll figure it out."

"So this isn't a marriage proposal?" he suggested.

"No."

"Just a holdup for money."

She flinched again but refused to deny his charge. "Yes."

He gulped the rest of his coffee and put the cup back in the saucer with a clink. "How much?"

She stared, confused, her mind still churning from all the emotions that were bubbling to the surface.

"How much money?" His voice was a growl.

"I—I don't know."

"You haven't thought this out much, have you?" he ridiculed softly. He didn't move but she felt as if he were almost in her lap, cutting off her breath. "Or did you think that I might come up with more money if I figured it out myself?"

She shook her head, denying his claim. Her eyes were wide and she knew he saw the tears that still threatened to fall. She didn't have the ability to hide it anymore.

"Give me a ballpark figure," he prompted, his voice softening.

"The medical bills shouldn't be more than a thousand or so; my hospitalization will pick up the rest. I'll need about five hundred before the baby comes. I'm getting a salary until August. But I won't be able to go back to teaching this fall semester. . . ." She hesitated, drawing a shaking hand through her mahogany-dark hair. She gathered her scattered thoughts together as she searched for the figures he demanded. "About six hundred a month for six months after the baby is born."

"About five thousand, give or take a hundred," Adam murmured.

She gulped as she heard the sum. She hadn't added up the numbers before but it was almost a third of her yearly paycheck. Maybe she could cut back somehow. But how? "I'll be working before the baby comes. . . ."

"Either way, it's a high price tag for one night in a hotel room with a woman I barely knew. An expensive lesson in life."

Her throat closed up on unshed tears. "For both of us."

Pushing his cup away, he leaned over the table. "If I agree to this, I call the shots, Marissa." His tone intimidated her even more than his actions. "You want five thousand from me; that entitles me to something."

Her eyes couldn't leave his as she stared into what must certainly be the edge of hell. And hell was cold—not hot. She looked at him with confusion in her eyes. "What shots? What 'something'?" Her voice was barely a whisper.

He stretched back in his chair again and a sigh of relief escaped her. "I'm not sure yet. I'll let you know."

"When?"

"Soon." Adam gazed at her as he reached into his breast pocket and pulled out a small appointment book. "What's your telephone number and address?"

She gave it, her voice quivering. The situation would have been funny if it hadn't been so tragic. She was pregnant by a man who didn't even know how to get in touch with her.

He slipped the book back into his pocket. "Why?" he questioned quietly. "Why did you go to bed with me? You practically threw yourself at me the night of the party."

Because I love you. She shook her head. "I don't know. I just don't know." Her actions were jerky as she lifted her cup to lips that almost refused to move. "Why did you take me to your bed?"

Adam stood, his shadow towering over her. Withdrawing his wallet, he threw a five-dollar bill on the table. His eyes were cold and the color of slate. "You were available."

Pain coursed through every part of her body, paralyzing her with its intensity. When she opened her eyes, he was gone.

Her shoulders slumped. Despite the crowd surrounding her, she dropped her head to her hands and cried silent tears.

It was several minutes later that she realized she still didn't know what he was going to do. Adam had never said he would help.

ADAM STRODE toward the Galleria parking garage. His steps were quick and decisive, but his mind was in a hell of a mess. He was going to be a father, and he hadn't even known the mother's address or telephone number until ten minutes ago. Terrific. His father would love it. At least his mother wasn't around to see this happen. She'd have been clamoring about marriage and commitment as if it were the problem solver of the century. But, hell, the woman had never faced the fact that her own husband had cheated behind her back more times than Houston had people. If nothing else, his parents' marriage had brought home the lesson of monogamy—and how seldom it worked in real life. It was nothing but a myth, a fantasy that most women believed and most men were trapped in. He had learned that fact when he was a child at his father's knee.

It was a lesson well learned until now. When he was a teenager and not as discriminating when it came to available females, he had wondered if this would ever happen to him. He'd had his life so well mapped out that he had been more careful than most of his peers.

Always cautious—until one night when there'd been just enough liquor and not enough sense. He'd gotten caught, and that mistake was about to change his whole life. It wasn't a question of money, but of his own self-image.

Marissa. Marissa was pregnant with his child. He was staggered by the enormity of his actions one night three months ago.

After living together for three years, he and Elizabeth had broken up following a battle royal on the same topic. She wanted marriage and a baby. He didn't. It was the perfect excuse to end a relationship he'd been drifting in for a long time and didn't want to continue with, anyway. What he hadn't liked was that she'd broken it off before he had thought it through. That had happened just days before the infamous alumni party—and Marissa.

He'd been working night and day on a project that, if it had worked, would have made him a millionaire three times over. Instead it had burned to ashes that week, almost sending him to the poorhouse. His ego was crushed by both Elizabeth's demands and the fact that he had made a wrong—very wrong—business decision. Then there appeared sweet Marissa, ready to soothe his ravaged ego and give him the moment of peace he desperately needed before starting to pick up the pieces and glue his life back together.

The breakup with Elizabeth had hurt his pride at the time—as if she had betrayed their original agreement—but while days passed into weeks, he'd come to hardly notice she wasn't there. No more mess in the house, no more parties he didn't want to attend. No more exorbitant cleaning bills and even more exorbitant clothing bills. In fact, a month after she had left he had to admit to himself that he was enjoying the peace. And the anger quickly disappeared, like smoke. Love wasn't involved; they'd merely become a habit that hadn't been all that hard to break.

But less than one week after the breakup and during his business crisis had come the alumni party—and the night with Marissa. He'd known her socially as a Little Sister in a fraternity he had belonged to in his college days. Little Sisters helped put on parties and made arrangements for the boys who weren't as well versed in the social amenities. Although Marissa had been a part of those yearly postgrad get-togethers, he'd purposely stayed away from her. She was too sweet, too pretty, too young. But his good intentions had gone to hell in a hand basket three months ago.

Even though he hated to admit it, he deserved more than half the blame for that night. He'd been angry and frustrated with the world in general. And a couple of drinks had only added to his gloomy self-pity. If he had been in his right mind, he would have taken precautions, but who in the hell could have guessed that Marissa wasn't sexually active and aware of the responsibility required for the act? Every other woman he had ever met was!

He didn't doubt for a moment that he was the father of her child. Looking back, all kinds of warning bells had gone off, but in his need, he'd ignored them.

He edged behind the steering wheel of his Alfa Romeo with Marissa's image dancing in his mind. Her brown eyes were so big they almost swallowed her face. Her tiny figure was still slight despite the fact that she was carrying his baby. And the entire time they'd been talking, her beautifully shaped hands were trembling all the way up to her elbows.

Marissa could have been the world's most desirable woman, but Adam Pierce still didn't want a wife. His conscience prickled at that thought—she hadn't asked him to marry her. She only wanted monetary help, and not even much of that.

He turned the key in the ignition. It was time to visit his attorney. Maybe Mike would have a clue as to the next move. Putting the car in gear, Adam backed out of the parking space and headed toward Mike Butler's office. There were so many answers he needed and so much to do. . . .

MARISSA STEPPED INSIDE her apartment and silently thanked God for air conditioning. It was early July and the sun was already blistering. She felt more like a limp piece of lettuce than a soon-to-be-mother—except for being nauseous; that seemed to be a constant reminder. The doctor had promised that her stomach would settle down as time passed, but so far no luck. She woke up every morning, ate a ton of saltine crackers, and then threw up. It was becoming a ritual. Wonderful fun, this pregnancy thing.

Still, since her pregnancy had been confirmed and become fact, she wouldn't have it any other way. For her there had been no alternative, although she had certainly logically reviewed them all. Subconsciously, she'd made her choice the instant she had realized she was pregnant. This was her baby, and unless things absolutely overwhelmed her, she was keeping it. She and the baby would share the same future, whatever that might be.

She stretched out on the small couch in her minuscule living room and prayed her stomach would settle down. This particular bout of nausea could be attributed to the confrontation she had just gone through with Adam, she thought.

Adam.

How naive she had been! He'd visited the fraternity house several times over the years, and from afar, she had nursed a crush on him. She treasured every word, gesture and smile directed at her with the same longing that drove other girls to fantasize that movie stars spoke to them personally through the silver screen.

And he had hardly known she existed until that night three months ago. He'd been sitting in a corner, drinking, ignoring all the friends who usually congregated around him. Rumor had it that a big oil deal he'd been working on had just flopped. He looked as if were heading for a hangover, so gathering her nerve, she'd poured a glass of tonic, added a twist of lemon and handed it to him, thinking that he might not notice the lack of liquor. Instead, he'd noticed her. And when he did, she was foolish enough to believe she'd found the doorway to heaven.

If that wasn't irony! Heaven turned out to be heaving into a commode, thanks to her own misguided sense of purpose.

So now she was pregnant and losing her job as a junior-high earth-sciences teacher. No school was going to allow her to teach when she was pregnant and unmarried. That was a state some of her students found themselves in, even in junior high. What a shining example to set for them! Once the baby was born she'd move to another school district and pretend she was divorced, but for now, she knew she had to hand in her resignation so they could seek a replacement for the fall term. The baby was due at Christmas. Ho, ho, ho. Merry Christmas.

Her stomach roiled and she took a deep breath, trying to ease the tension that flowed from her aching head to her stiff toes. Easy. . . Easy does it.

Closing her eyes, she pretended she was on a tropical isle without a problem in the world. Ever so slowly, her body responded, beginning to relax. Thank goodness tomorrow was Sunday and she had all day to sleep, another thing she did a lot of lately. . . .

The jangling phone startled her and she sat up too quickly. She grabbed her stomach with one hand while reaching for the receiver with the other. "Hello?"

"Marissa? Adam." He sounded so cool and nononsense. A businessman through and through. "When is the baby due?"

Nothing like getting to the point. "December."

"December what?"

"December twenty-eight," she said tiredly. "Why?"

"If I'm the father, shouldn't I know?"

"Yes, of course. I'm sorry."

"What's the name of your apartment complex?"

She told him and was met with silence from the other end. Pressing the phone closer to her ear, she heard another voice softly talking. Who was with him? Elizabeth?

Then he spoke clearly in her ear. "You're moving. Next week. Pick a day."

Her stomach tensed and roiled again. "No, I'm *not* moving. I'm staying right where I am. The rent is cheap and the building is close to my job," she stated firmly. "Don't try to take over my life, Adam. Just say whether or not you'll help me."

"You'd love for me to say I won't help, wouldn't you? Then you could take me to court and prove I'm the father. After that I could wind up paying child support for the next twenty-one years." His voice was filled with bitterness. "Besides, Marissa, you no longer have a job. Remember?"

"My memory is very good, Adam. How could I forget that night of bliss?" she retorted angrily. "Your bliss, not mine, I might add."

The tension passed from her nerves to her muscles, cramping her whole body with the action. Her anger left but she knew she had transferred it to him, by the silence on the other end of the line. She felt compelled to fill it. "I'm not asking for twenty-one years of support; just one year and then we're free of each other." Her stomach clenched as bile rose to her throat. A cold sweat popped out on her forehead and she covered her mouth with her hand. "Oh, lord, no," she moaned, dropping the phone on the couch and running to the bathroom. She could hear Adam shouting her name, but for the life of her there was nothing she could do except continue on her path.

By the time the spasms had stopped and she had wiped her forehead with a damp washcloth a good five minutes had passed. Cautiously she picked up the phone again and listened. No dial tone, no busy signal. Nothing.

"Hello?"

"Marissa?"

"Yes?"

"This is Mike Butler. I'm Adam's attorney. Are you all right?"

She laughed shakily. "I'm fine. I just had a meaningful relationship with John, that's all."

"John? Is someone else there?"

She chuckled again. "No, the commode. My stomach hasn't been in the best of form lately," she confessed, then smiled to herself. What an understatement that was! She could hardly think, let alone adjust to the changes in her body chemistry.

"I see." He was embarrassed, but she was too tired to care. "Well, Adam should be there any moment. He thought someone might have broken into the apartment."

Mike had no sooner spoken than there was a banging on the door. "Marissa! Are you in there? Open up!" Adam's voice came through so loudly that the sound probably zinged through everyone else's door, too. "Marissa!"

"His master's voice," she said into the receiver. "Just a moment."

Adam looked as she felt—slightly panicked and more than a little bit irritated. "What in hell happened?" he asked as he stormed four steps into the apartment, then stopped dead in his tracks when he realized that another step would take him into the world's smallest kitchen, bypassing the world's smallest living room. He turned around, spotted the phone and pointed to it. "Is that Mike?"

She nodded, closing the door and leaning against the cool wood. She was too tired to move back to the couch. Her whole body felt as if it were made of wet sponge. She watched him through half-closed lids as he talked, then listened to his attorney. Apparently the conversation had to do with her, but she couldn't work up enough interest to care.

Whatever was said, by the time Adam hung up he was calmer. "Sit down before you fall down," he ordered, but his voice was almost soft.

She moved to obey, but her hand didn't want to let go of the doorknob. She could have taken shouting or anger, but consideration—especially from him—completely unnerved her. Throughout the past three months no one had cared about her. Not really.

He muttered a curse under his breath as he helped her to the couch and sat her at one end. Even though he settled at the other end, when he turned toward her his knee almost touched hers. "You're making yourself sick." His declaration made her smile.

"No," she said. "The baby is. But the doctor promises that both the depression and the nausea will go away."

"Who's your doctor?"

"Jane Brody. On Westheimer."

"When did you last see her?"

She leaned her head back against the couch and closed her eyes. "Four weeks ago, when she ran the tests and confirmed what I already knew."

Through a dim fog she heard him dial the phone and carry on a conversation. Then all was quiet. . . .

ADAM STARED at the sleeping woman. She looked like a vulnerable child herself. So many emotions flowed through him he couldn't distinguish one from another. That wasn't quite true. One response stood out from all the rest: protectiveness.

Elizabeth was classically elegant, possessing the same flawless beauty as a marble statue or a cool watercolor painting. But Marissa was beautiful, too, in a different way—a wholesome way. Her skin was clear except for the light sprinkling of freckles across the bridge of her nose. Her lashes were naturally long and slightly curled. Her mouth was full and curved to form a bow shape, which probably accounted for her air of vulnerability. She had none of the sophistication that other women he'd known had worn like an enveloping cloak. Just by looking at her, he should have known Marissa would be trouble.

He stared at her stomach as if he could see the baby there. Black slacks and a baggy black sweater hid any sign of pregnancy. She looked just the same as she had three months ago, except for the light violet smudges under her eyes.

Mike said she had been throwing up. Leaning back on the couch, he ran a hand through his hair. He had to figure out how to take care of her for the next year.

His gaze roved over the small apartment. Eventually she was going to have to move. And since he owned two apartment complexes and a high-rise condominium, he should be able to find a spot for her somewhere. After all, Houston's economy was such that his occupancy rates were already below seventy percent.

He stood, refusing to tackle another problem until Marissa awoke and he could deal directly with the woman who had the nerve to turn his life upside down.

Mike was drawing up the papers that she would be required to sign before they went any further with this farce. All that was left was to see what kind of a woman was going to be the mother of his child. If he liked her, he would be generous. If he didn't—well, that would be easy, too. And if she wasn't fit for anything, he'd dump her and take the child to raise himself. Not that he knew anything about children, but it wasn't the poor kid's fault that he was an accident. . . .

Marriage was out of the question—not just from his point of view but apparently from hers, too, if her reaction today was any indication. Thank goodness. He'd stayed single for thirty-two years and wanted to remain so. There was nothing he'd seen in his or his parents' relationships or his friends' marriages that had changed his mind lately.

He glanced into her bedroom. It didn't hold much. A twin bed, a dresser she had obviously painted herself and a small desk piled with papers and books were the only furniture, which was a good thing because this room was on as small a scale as the rest of the apartment. But the feeling of the place was restful; she had decorated with posters of plants and scenic woodlands. He stared at the twin bed. Obviously what she had said about not having been with other men was true, for no two people could sleep comfortably there. Of course, she might go to the man's apartment. . . .

It didn't matter. He was still at fault. He knew it deep down inside, without all the folderol of logic.

So now he had to pay the piper.

He had the feeling that the price was going to be much greater than five thousand dollars, give or take a hundred. . . .

2

MARISSA'S CHIN JUTTED UPWARD. "Read my lips. I...am...not...mov-ing." She stood defiantly, toe-to-toe, with the most bullheaded, obstinate man she had ever met. Her brown eyes flashed specks of golden flame. He was much taller than her almost five-foot-two, and her neck ached from looking up at him but she refused to retreat from her aggressive stance. "My rent is paid until the end of the month and I don't have money to throw away—unlike you, Mr. Pierce."

He raised a questioning brow, apparently unperturbed by her outburst. "Don't you think it's a little silly to call me that now?"

"To love you is to know you?" Her tone was sweetly scalding.

"It wasn't love, it was sex," he snapped back, his control finally beginning to slip. "And apparently one-sided satisfaction, as you so succinctly pointed out earlier."

Quelling the grin of satisfaction on hearing that her gibe had hit home, she waved one petite hand in the air, erasing his words. "None of that matters now. What *does* matter is that you're trying to take over my life. And *that*, Adam Pierce, I won't have."

He crossed his arms and glared down at her as if she were an ant invading his picnic. "And how will you stop me? You have bills to pay and a baby to care for, to say nothing of taking better care of yourself. Without my help, what will you do?"

He saw a flash of fear darken her big eyes. He wanted to smile in triumph, but it was too soon. Then she straightened. "I don't know," she finally admitted. "But I came to you for help, not for leadership. If necessary, I'll think of something."

"Give up the baby?" He was goading her and he knew it. He just couldn't stop. She was so damned feisty, and he wasn't used to having someone else calling the shots. He usually called the tune or didn't dance at all. Besides, he was enjoying the fight.

She narrowed her eyes, reminding him of a kitten spitting at a lion. He almost grinned at the imagery. "You'd like that, wouldn't you? Then your end of the responsibility—and your money—would be safe."

He held back his laughter. She acted as if she were requesting an enormous sum. And it probably was, to her. That last thought killed the grin that had tried to form. "I don't give a damn, lady. You came to me and I told you at the time that if I agreed we would have to do it my way. This is my way."

"You mean you won't help unless I move?" she looked at him incredulously.

Adam nodded.

"But that's crazy! It would cost more money to move! The rent would be higher, the utilities more, and the telephone would have to be relocated. And they charge for all that. The move would cost too much!"

"I can handle it."

"On top of the five thousand?" Her voice squeaked.

"Yes. I may even throw in the utilities, since you'll be moving into a building I own."

Suddenly it all made sense. She'd be moving to one of his apartments. She could have kicked herself for not realizing that sooner. But then she hadn't been thinking clearly lately. She'd just bet there was a way he could write off the expense on income tax and come out ahead in the bargain. "Of course," she murmured, suddenly docile. Her eyes flicked up to his, then back to the floor. "Okay, I give in. When does this move take place?"

"Tomorrow."

"That's Sunday. No moving company will move on a Sunday."

"This one will."

The tone of voice gave her the clue. "Don't tell me," she said, turning to flop down on the couch. "You own a moving company."

He shrugged, suddenly looking uncomfortable. "With so many apartments, it made good business sense to have a moving company. And for your information, most people move out of apartments on the weekend. They work during the week."

He glanced around the small, tastefully but sparsely furnished space. "Are you sure you want to take this stuff? You could always rent some furniture."

"This is mine, all bought and paid for," she stated firmly. "I'm taking it."

For the first time since he had barged into her apartment, he grinned. "All right. I just asked."

"Where am I moving to?"

"Two Twenty-two Towers." He turned and stared out the wide window at the courtyard. Two children played on their tricycles below, riding around and around a stairwell post.

"I can't." Her voice was soft and full of fear.

He tore his eyes away from the scene and stared at her, his brow furrowing. "What do you mean, you can't? I thought we just went through all this?"

"Those condominiums are for sale, right?"

He nodded, his eyes still showing the question he had originally asked.

"They cost more in one month than a year's rent on this apartment and then some. You'll lose money by putting me in one. You should keep it open to sell, not give it away."

The grin he'd tried to kill earlier came back. "I'll suffer the loss gracefully."

"If you put me in one of the other apartments, there won't be such a loss. Then we can both live with ourselves without recriminations."

"I promise I'll never throw it up at you," he said, wondering if he was reading her correctly. She was acting more worried about his finances than he was! His eyes narrowed. Was this a game? A scam she was much better at than he? "Now go freshen up. We're going over there now so you can see the place. Afterward we'll eat."

"No."

He stared at her. "What do you mean, 'No'?" he finally gritted through his teeth, perfectly willing to shake her until some of his pent-up frustration was gone.

"I mean I'd love to see the condo, but I won't have dinner with you tonight."

"Why not?"

"Because I don't feel like being in your company for hours at a time. I want to come home and be by myself for a while." Her words were spoken softly, but her eyes told the rest of the story. She was exhausted.

He sighed heavily. "Fine. Let's go."

Marissa fastened her seat belt and stared out her window, determined not to look at the man who climbed into the bucket seat next to her. The lump in her throat told her she wanted to cry again, and she swallowed hard to erase it.

"Are you all right?" he asked before turning the key in the ignition.

"Fine," she managed. This afternoon's confrontation with Adam had been hell. And it had come on the heels of their meeting at the Galleria, when she had told him of their "problem." It was enough for one day...one week . . . one lifetime.

She wanted him to leave her alone. Perversely, she also wanted him to wrap her in his arms, hold her close to his heart and soothe her ragged spirit by persuading her everything would be all right and he would stand by her. Her battling emotions didn't make any sense, and the confusion just added to the depression clouding her mind.

They edged down a well-traveled street and she glanced at her watch. Five o'clock. Traffic time. Her eyes darted to both sides of the road. She wouldn't admit it, but she was looking forward to seeing the inside of Adam's condominium. She had heard of Two Twenty-two Towers—everybody had. It was one of the best addresses in the city. Her heart beat a little faster. Apparently curiosity was a strong energizer.

Adam pulled off the main thoroughfare and wheeled onto a small side street lined with shade trees. Adam's building occupied the entire left-hand side of the next block. It was tall—at least thirty stories—and the lines were simple but beautiful. Marissa thought it looked like a sleek, smooth sculpture, and she had the urge to touch it with her palms, to feel the sensuous curves for herself.

The front entrance was protected by a deep blue awning, the smoked-glass doors only allowing a glimpse of an enormous chandelier in the lobby. Adam turned into the drive, then steered the car down into the underground parking. She swiveled to see the well-lit garage complex. The walls were color coded in shades of green, blue, orange, red and yellow, apparently directing residents where to park. At the end of the entryway stood a guard in uniform, his smile as big as the state. He gave a mock salute, then raised the gate for Adam to drive through.

"Normally you stick your key card in that machine and the block will rise. The guard is here only in case there's a problem."

"Of course," she murmured dryly, hoping he couldn't hear the awe she felt right down to her toes.

They parked directly next to the elevator in a slot marked Reserved. He turned off the key. "You'll park in this slot instead of your condo slot."

"Why?"

"You have to question everything I say, don't you?"

"Only when you give orders I'm expected to follow," she warned. "I won't do anything blindly, Adam."

He sighed heavily, hinting that his patience was almost at an end. "Parking there means you won't have to walk to the elevator. And if you have groceries, you'll park in the circular drive above. The guys at the front desk will bring your groceries upstairs and park your car for you."

"Of course." She stepped out before he could open her door for her, hoping he got the message that she preferred being a liberated female who didn't need his help.

His look told her that although he let her get away with it this time, he didn't agree. She gave a sigh. This wasn't going to be easy. But then she should have known that anything to do with Adam Pierce wasn't going to be a snap.

Adam placed the coded card into a slot in the elevator wall. The doors whooshed closed and the elevator began its silent assent. It stopped on the twenty-eighth floor and the doors opened to display a spacious, tastefully decorated sitting area with two couches and several tables, one of which held a large Chinese vase filled with delicate silk apple blossoms.

Champagne-white carpeting stretched down the hallway, and Marissa followed Adam's footsteps as he led her on the path toward the end. Swiveling cameras were placed strategically on the walls, ensuring security even in the corridors. They reached the last door and he slid a key in the lock and the cream-colored double doors opened with a soft click.

Marissa stood at his side thinking that this wasn't possible. Not possible at all.

Adam pushed open the doors and disclosed a brick wall that gave privacy to the room beyond. "This is a two-bedroom, two-bath unit," he explained as he rounded the brick partition, which she realized was actually the back side of a fireplace. Without allowing her to stop, he led her into a wide expanse of living room. To the left and up one step was the dining room. One wall was mirrored so it could repeat the spectacular view provided by the windows that spanned the entire length of the rooms.

Downtown Houston with its distinctive modern skyline could be seen straight ahead, the Texas Medical Center's tall buildings were to the right and the Galleria area, looking much like a new downtown all on it's own, surrounded them.

Marissa walked to the window and stared out, folding her arms in front of her to hide her nervousness. How had all this happened? And when had she lost control of the situation?

Adam stood next to her, pocketing the key. He motioned toward the left side of the room. "That's the kitchen, breakfast area and utility room. And over there—" he pointed to the two doors against the far right wall "—are the bedrooms. There's a full bath and a half between them and a half bath behind the dining room."

Her breath was light and quickened with each intake of air. This was out of her league. She would never fit into this place or this life-style. Taking a deep breath, she faced him. "I can't move in here."

"Why not?" His gray eyes focused on her and she took a step back.

"Because this is—this . . ." She couldn't find the right words.

"Too little? Too big? Not the right color scheme?"

"Too much."

He frowned. "Too much what?"

She shrugged. "Too much . . . everything."

He stepped closer. "Marissa, look at me." He spoke quietly, but his voice was laced with steel. Against her will, she did as she was told and saw the chill seeping into his gaze.

"There is nothing wrong with this unit. There is nothing wrong with you living in it. In fact, it's the only way I'll be sure that you're safe and well cared for. A restaurant on the top floor will cater your meals when or if you're not feeling well. The small restaurant on the ground floor will serve you breakfast whenever you want it. Security guards are here to ensure your safety from car to apartment. A complete gym, swimming pool, sauna and racquetball courts are downstairs in the basement so you can stay in shape. There are bell-hops in the lobby who will make sure you don't strain yourself if you need something moved or carried." He hesitated, then continued in a softer tone. "And I live in the penthouse, in case of emergency."

The only escape valve left to her was anger. "Oh? Is this supposed to be like having a mistress on hand in case you need one? Is that what all this is about?" Her hands dug into her hips. "This place must cost thousands a month. Isn't that rather a high price tag for a playmate? Especially a very *reluctant* one?"

"Too bad you've only now realized the value of reluctance." He made a lingering appraisal of her figure, his gaze returning to the rise and fall of her breasts. Electricity crackled between them as Marissa felt her body flush in response to his glance. "First of all, you've already set the price, and five thousand every time I want to make love to you is a trifle high, even in my books. Second, I don't think you'll be all that sexy in another month or so." He pointedly lowered his eyes to the slight roundness of her stomach.

His words were well-aimed darts that hit her vulnerability. She felt her cheeks redden and closed her eyes to hide her humiliation. She was embarrassed by her own words; she'd been a fool to strike out at him. Who was she kidding? She'd played the fool from the moment she'd met him!

His voice was soft and soothing as he continued. "This condo is empty and will remain empty even if you don't move in. But a tenant, even though she doesn't pay, is good business."

Her eyes were still closed. "Would you like me to find a few good friends to help you fill the rest? I'm sure it could be arranged."

"Male or female?" His teasing voice sent a shiver down Marissa's spine. He was kind when he wanted to be, and such a stinker the rest of the time.

She opened her eyes and got lost in the grayness of his. "Both," she said hoarsely.

He shook his head slowly, a smile tugging at the corners of his lips. "No, thanks. One tenant with the stubbornness of a giant mule is all I'm capable of coping with." He took her arm and steered her toward the bedrooms, his fingers scalding her skin. "At least for the moment."

From the master bedroom French doors opened onto a spacious patio just itching to hold plants and comfortable lawn furniture. In the far corner of the balcony was an outdoor closet for storage of just such items.

"Beautiful," she murmured as he led her through to one of the largest bathrooms she had ever seen. Double sinks and an oversize, all-glass shower stall were at one end of the large room. Two closets large enough to be bedrooms were at either end of the bath. But the focal point of the room was the jetted tub. It sat up on a dais in front of a stained-glass window that sent shards of rainbow-colored light everywhere. The effect was that of delightfully decadent intimacy.

"Fit for Nero," she murmured.

"You mean for an orgy?" he whispered teasingly in her ear. Laughter edged his voice.

"I mean this room was designed by a perverted mind." She hoped that shot hit home.

"Thank you."

The other bedroom was smaller, but Marissa decided that small was in the eye of the beholder. It was almost as large as her entire apartment.

He ushered her out the bedroom door and toward the entrance. "I'll have the moving crew at your place around nine tomorrow," he said, closing the apartment doors behind them and walking her toward the elevators."

"But I can't pack everything between now and then!"

"You won't have to," he assured her calmly. "They'll pack everything for you, including the dishes and your clothing. All you have to do is watch them work."

Stepping into the elevator after her, he pushed the lobby button. When he noticed her puzzled look, he explained. "You only need the card from the garage entrance. If you come through the lobby, the elevator works as usual."

She nodded, wondering tiredly if she would ever remember all this. She was out of her league and knew it; she just didn't know what to do about it. Adam Pierce was storming through her life wearing hobnail boots. And she couldn't think of a single way to stop him.

The lobby was all golden-brown marble, expensive furniture and Oriental rugs. A wrap around desk squatted on the left side of the room where a uniformed guard was perched on an upholstered bar stool watching miniature TV screens that showed all the hallways. A bellboy stood to one side, sorting through mail and slotting letters into their proper places.

"Pete, Arnold, I want you to meet a new tenant, Marissa Madison. She'll be on the twenty-eighth floor, number nine."

Both men were polite and highly respectful. And both eyed her with unconcealed curiosity. "Jesse told me you were here, Mr. Pierce, even before I saw you on the monitor," Pete said after the introductions were made. "He said to remind you that the movers will need some information from you."

A look passed between the two men and Adam nodded. "Right." He glanced toward the younger man. "Arnold, if you see Miss Madison with packages or anything else that she shouldn't be carrying by herself, you're to step in immediately. The same goes for deliveries. Take them up to her instead of letting her know by intercom."

"Yes, sir."

It wasn't until they were in the car and Marissa leaned her head back against the seat that she thought of what she wanted to ask. "Are there smaller apartments, Adam?"

"One or two." His voice was cautious.

"Could I have one of those instead?"

"No."

"Why?"

"Because when the baby comes, you'll need the larger space. And because I get to dictate a few things concerning the child's life."

"So far, that's *all* you've been doing," she said disgustedly, wanting to argue but feeling too tired to bother.

"That's the way it should be."

His smugness banished her exhaustion. She sat up and stared at him, her eyes filled with anger. "I am *not* some nameless, witless bimbo who needs to have a man in order to live, Adam Pierce. I have never been one and I refuse to start now!"

His brows shot up. "Have I done anything that was bad for you?"

She shook her head.

"Have I tried to harm you or the baby in any way?"

She shook her head again.

"Thank you. Then please shut up." She opened her mouth. "And if you have anything to say, Marissa, it had better be constructive criticism or an honest opinion. Anything said just to cause aggravation will be considered an act of war."

She closed her mouth. What was the use? She'd think of all the right things to say tomorrow—after a good night's sleep.

THE NEXT MORNING was just like any other morning. The alarm went off at seven, she ate nine saltine crackers, silently cursed her weakness and then added new curses for Adam. No sense leaving out the father and partner in crime, especially since he seemed so anxious to get involved.

She refused to think about how handsome he was, or how his face creased into a grin that made her blood sing through her veins. That was what had got her into this mess to begin with. Besides, he didn't care for her. She told herself it should be enough that he was kind and helpful . . . but deep down inside, she knew that it wasn't.

"Greedy girl," she muttered, turning over to form a tight ball in the hope that her stomach would believe she was still asleep.

It didn't work. At eight o'clock Marissa made her daily trip to the side of the commode—again cursing. By the time she had showered and dressed, the crew Adam had sent to move her had arrived.

"Is this it, lady?" The man in charge looked around as if she had nothing in the room.

She followed his gaze. "This is it. Why?"

He kept looking down at his clipboard and then back up at the apartment as if he couldn't quite believe his orders. "We brought a truck big enough for furniture from a two-bedroom apartment. This doesn't look like enough stuff to fill a ten-by-ten U-Haul."

She sipped her first cup of coffee of the day and ignored the implied insult. Giving her best imitation of a bimbo, she smiled and sat down cross-legged on the couch. Blinking, she stared wide-eyed at the three men standing in the doorway as if they were Larry, Moe and Curly and were here to put on a show.

The man in charge heaved a sigh of resignation and said, "Okay, guys. Get the boxes and let's start packin'."

Adam was right. When he had dropped her off last night he had told her not to interfere with the men and they'd get the job done in no time.

Once started, it took them less than an hour to box her things and another hour to load them. She stood on the sidewalk and stared at the truck, forcing back tears. Everything she'd worked for in the past four years was in that moving van. It was the sum total of her life, all boxed now because of a mistake made three months ago. . . .

"Missing it already?" Adam stood beside her and she hadn't noticed his arrival.

Yes, she was. The hair on the back of her neck had prickled, but she had ignored the sensation, chalking it up to the emotional roller coaster she seemed to be on these days. She didn't trust any of her senses lately. "Just watching. You told me that was all I could do."

He gave her a dry look. "How obedient."

She shrugged, plunging her hands into the back pockets of her jeans.

"Have you talked to the apartment manager?"

She nodded. "Tomorrow I'll get my mail forwarded and have the telephone switched over, but everything else is taken care of."

"Good." He placed a hand on her elbow and led her toward his car. "Let's go."

"Where?"

"To get something to eat and then to check out the guys at the apartment."

"I've got to do some grocery shopping first," she protested, her steps balking. "And I can't leave my car here."

"No problem. I'll help with the shopping and we're having breakfast at the condo restaurant." He turned toward the men clanging the doors shut on the back of the truck. "Hey, Smitty! Take that yellow Volkswagen with you."

The man's face held a knowing look. "Sure thing, boss. Where's the key?"

Reluctantly Marissa handed her keys to Adam and he threw them to Smitty. She gave a sharp sigh as she settled into the marshmallow-leather seat and watched Adam move around the front of the car. What else could she do but follow his orders right now? She could argue about wanting to drive the Volkswagen herself, but she'd only wind up losing. Adam was in charge and couldn't begin to understand her hesitancy to have him take over her life. Besides, there were other, more important points she needed to win. A trite saying her mother used to quote came back to her: don't win the battle just to lose the war.

Adam slipped into the driver's seat and put the key in the ignition. His hand dropped to his jeans-clad thigh. "Marissa?"

Large brown eyes filled with confusion turned toward him, making his gut clench in reaction. He cursed softly under his breath. Reaching out, he curved his hand around the slimness of her neck. "Try not to worry. It'll all work out."

"I never should have asked for your help," she whispered.

"Why?"

"Because you're like a tornado that whirls in and sweeps up everything in its path. When you leave I won't know where anything is or what I should do next.

You're swallowing me alive, Adam. And I don't know what to do about it."

He gently caressed her neck. "Stop me."

"How?"

"Tell me."

She smiled sadly. "Stop, Adam. You're taking over my life, my decisions, my breath."

He leaned back on the headrest. "What do you *not* want me to do?" His fingertips grazed her cheek.

She tried to ignore his touch by focusing on his words. "Make my decisions. *Ask* me if I want my car driven. *Ask* me if I want breakfast or lunch or dinner. *Ask* me if you can go shopping with me."

"Is it okay if Smitty drives your car?"

She nodded.

"Are you hungry? Would you like a bit of lunch before we check on your furniture?"

Her stomach growled in answer and she chuckled ruefully, drawing a smile from him. "Yes, please. I'd love to."

"Then, if it's all right with you, perhaps I could show you where the nearest markets, shopping center and pharmacy are so you'll be able to find your way around the neighborhood by yourself in the future."

"I'd like that."

His gaze was caught by the slight indentation on either side of her full mouth—small parentheses that highlighted her smiles. Funny. He hadn't noticed before. He shook himself. "Then it's settled," he muttered, finally dropping his hand from her neck to the key. "I don't see what the fuss was all about, Marissa. You were going to say yes to all those things anyway."

She grinned as she sat back and relaxed. "But you didn't know that until you asked, Mr. Pierce."

He whipped the steering wheel around and entered the busy street traffic, his mind in turmoil.

When Marissa had confronted him with "their" problem he had felt stunned, but that shock had soon turned to guilt. Because she hadn't asked for much, he had decided to help her all he could. Up until a moment ago, he was pretty proud of the way he'd handled things—and himself. But now he wasn't sure if he should have done anything other than what she'd requested.

He had a feeling that Marissa Madison was going to turn his life around in more ways than he had dreamed possible. And that was the root of his dilemma. He should have been upset by her turning his life upside down. Instead, he was reacting to the one thing that never failed to intrigue him: the headiness of a challenge.

3

MARISSA CLOSED HER EYES and leaned against the wall as the elevator steadily rose to her floor. The gesture had more to do with blocking out Adam's presence than her being tired. But he wouldn't let her forget him that easily. He rattled the packages in his arms as he shifted the load for easier balance.

When the doors opened, she stood straight and began the long trek down the hall and toward her apartment. The door was open; apparently the moving men were still there.

What greeted her was almost comical.

The three uniformed men stood in the middle of the room, staring at the space her furniture *didn't* fill. There was more than enough of it.

"The room's a little bigger than I thought," Adam mused, but the mischief in his eyes belied any sympathy that she thought was due her.

"How am I supposed to make this warehouse space into a home without spending a fortune?"

All eyes were on her dismayed expression, and all with different emotions showing: amusement, consternation, sympathy and even helplessness in the face of what was surely a monumental task.

Adam spoke first. "Buy more furniture?"

Smitty spoke next. "Cover the carpet with scatter rugs? My Missus always did like scatter rugs."

"How about some plants?" one of the younger men suggested hopefully.

"I'd move," the other man said flatly. "I'm not that much in love with heights anyway."

"Right," Marissa drawled over her shoulder as she walked toward the kitchen to deposit the bags in her arms. "I'll take that into consideration."

"Take what into consideration?" Adam was right behind her.

"All of the above."

"I'll let the men go," he sat his packages next to hers on the counter.

"Thanks." But her reluctant mutter wasn't heard. He'd already turned and left the kitchen for the living room.

Within moments the apartment was empty of men except for Adam. Ignoring him because she didn't know what else to do, she put away the groceries they had bought.

She knew the exact moment he came to stand in the doorway, but she refused to break the rhythm of her activity. "Would you care for a bologna sandwich?"

"I hate bologna."

"I love it. With lots and lots of mustard."

He leaned against the doorjamb, his hands in the pockets of his pants. "You just ate lunch."

She nodded, placing the cereal on the bottom shelf.

"Are you still hungry?"

"No. I just thought you might be."

"Marissa." His voice carried the implied command to stop and face him. She did, raising her brows in silent inquiry.

"Can we find a way to get along that won't infringe on either of our sensibilities?"

"You mean can we get along without purposely rubbing each other the wrong way?"

His mouth tightened. "Yes."

She tilted her head, her dark hair sliding to one side. "I don't know. Can we?"

"I'll try if you will."

She nodded her head slowly. "Okay. But from now on nothing gets done or put in motion without my knowledge or permission."

He raised one hand. "Scout's honor."

"Then we shouldn't have any problem." She wanted to laugh at that. Being around Adam was problem enough!

He pushed away from the doorway and took two steps toward her. Reaching out, he brushed away a strand of her silky hair. "No problems," he whispered, and his warm breath caressed her lips.

"Why Adam?" she whispered, her lips almost touching his. "Why did you *really* go to bed with me?"

His parted mouth compressed into a tight line. "Do we have to discuss this now?"

"I think so," she said, pulling back and leaning against the counter. Her heart was pounding against her ribs, but she wasn't sure if it was because of his nearness or because she didn't want to hear the answer to her own question. She took a deep breath. "You keep setting up new guidelines for this—this relationship, and I'm not sure I'm following them."

"What guidelines?"

"At different times and by different degrees, you're cool, insulting, warm, helpful—and now you're coming on to me."

His eyes narrowed. "Are you always this blunt?"

A small dimple appeared at the upper corner of her mouth. "I prefer to call it honest."

He ran a hand through his hair, then took a seat at the small kitchen table. The room was quiet as he stared at his hands resting in front of him, then his eyes pinned hers, and her breath caught in her throat. "Okay. That's fair. To answer your question, I don't know why I went to bed with you. You've always intrigued me, I guess. Ever since I first saw you at the first alumni party. You were making sandwiches and cutting them into triangles as if it were the most important job in the world. Your tongue was out, just barely touching your top lip, and I wondered what it would be like to kiss you."

Her eyes grew round. "You did? I didn't think you even noticed me!"

"Oh, I noticed, all right. As you sawed at the sandwiches your bottom moved enticingly from side to side." He smiled ruefully at the memory. "Then one of the guys told me you were the new Little Sister and I stayed away. You were too young for a big bad wolf like me."

She edged toward the chair across from him, sitting with her legs crossed as she leaned over the table. "Tell me more."

"There isn't much to tell. You were at all the functions, but I knew better than to get involved with someone so naive and so much younger than I was." He looked back down at his hands again, a frown marring his brow. "Until three months ago, that is, when you approached me. I was feeling pretty sorry for myself at the time. You always seemed so sympathetic toward everyone else, but every time I had ever approached you, you'd edged away as if I were poison. But that night, you came to comfort me." He shrugged. "I guess my common sense went on the blink."

"For both of us," she admitted. "My mother always told me to beware of men like you, but I was always more than a little fascinated by your kind; like a kid in front of a glowing fire, I wanted to touch the pretty colors instead of remembering that I could get burned."

He cocked his head, his gray eyes showing his curiosity. "Have you told your mother? You haven't mentioned your family."

She ran her hands under the thick hair at her neck, her fingers tangling in the riot of curls. When she glanced up, she found him watching her movements as if he wanted to feel the texture with his own hands. "My mother married my father because she was pregnant— with me." His eyes darted back to hers and she knew she had his attention. "I saw the misery a pregnancy combined with a forced marriage caused and swore I'd never find myself in the same situation. By the time I was fifteen I knew more about a woman's body and pregnancy than most adults know. By then, Mom and I had been on our own for a long time. Then she met my stepfather, Gar. Gar's first marriage was to a woman who had gotten pregnant, and he was bitter toward all women—all except his daughter and my best friend, Susanna. But the second time, Mom and Gar married for all the right reasons: love, respect, companionship and common interests. I gained a stepsister I love and we were a family for the first time ever.... So I learned both the pros and cons of marriage and love and sex."

"But you got caught anyway," he said softly.

She nodded. "Yes. I knew all the facts about sex, but I didn't realize how emotions could govern the act."

"Making love." His voice was firm as he corrected her.

"We weren't making love, Adam," she denied, a hint of regret in her voice. "Even you said so."

"Yes, we were. I lied. Whether love was a fleeting emotion or a more lasting one isn't the point. We still acted out of emotional need."

"Physical."

Anger flashed in his eyes. "Emotional."

"Why are you defending what we did?"

He sighed. "I don't know," he finally admitted, scraping back his chair and standing, his tall lean form dominating the room. "But I do know you look exhausted. How about taking a nap and I'll pick you up in time for dinner?"

"Thank you, but I'll eat here. I need time to get used to my new surroundings." She glanced around. "Funny, but I always thought that when I moved again, it would be into some little house that had a fenced backyard with a swing set and a sandbox."

"How domestic."

"Realistic. All children need space to move and play. And roots to feel sure of."

"Do you want a house instead of this?"

A feeling of hopelessness enveloped her. What good was a house? It still wouldn't be a home—not without love. She shrugged, turning away. "One place is as good as another."

His eyes narrowed. "I'll see you later tonight."

"Don't bother. Besides, I need to unpack."

"No, you don't. Everything's done. The men even emptied the boxes in your closet." He stepped out of the kitchen and toward the front door.

She began following him, reluctant to end their conversation even though she knew she was the one who asked for the reprieve. "Then I need to find the things they put away and arrange them my own way."

"All right," he conceded. "But have breakfast with me in the restaurant tomorrow. I need to get some information from you." Opening the door, he stood at the entrance, staring down at her tiny form.

"What for?"

"You'll find out tomorrow." He placed one finger on the small dimple that appeared as she returned his smile. His hand was warm and slightly callused—just as she remembered.

"See you then."

"Around eight." His voice was husky and a shiver of delight settled in her midsection.

"Right," she promised, then closed the door behind him and leaned against the jamb.

But her smile didn't leave.

ADAM LET HIMSELF into his apartment and threw the keys on the side table. It wasn't until he was in the kitchen making coffee that he realized he was whistling and had been ever since he left Marissa's apartment.

His whistling stopped.

The coffee began its steady drip into the pot and he watched it absently. Despite the hectic activity and the sudden upheaval in his life, he had thoroughly enjoyed the day. Marissa was responsible for that.

He had expected tears, recriminations and helpless, cloying femininity when he picked her up this morning. Instead, he'd found laughter, a sweet womanliness and sharp commentary mixed with common sense in equal doses. It was such a distinct difference from what he was used to that he was wary. Was her sweet independence an act that would soon collapse under its own strain?

The pot light came on and he poured a cup of coffee, then walked into the living room toward the bar. Opening a bottle of Kahlua, he poured a small amount into his cup and sat on the couch, staring out at the patio beyond.

He had to get himself under control. For a fleeting moment he had wondered what it would be like to live in a house with a big yard, with playing children making the noises that created contentment in a parent.

A house had always scared him, seeming more like a prison rooted to the ground than a place to live. He could easily move from apartment to apartment when he was dissatisfied, but a house—that required a sense of permanence. It was funny that others saw it as the ultimate happiness.

He leaned back and closed his eyes, almost afraid to delve too deeply into the satisfaction it gave him to know that Marissa was just two floors beneath him. There was so much to absorb. He was going to be a father in six months. Would he be active in the child's life or should he disappear and let Marissa do the raising? He pictured scenes of his son asking Marissa about his daddy and her trying to answer his questions. No, that wouldn't do. The child was his and would remain his. Period.

Listening to Marissa explain the bare essentials of her background today answered lots of small questions he had wondered about earlier. No wonder she didn't want marriage because of pregnancy; she'd seen what it could do to people. Did that mean that someday she would find a man whom she could love and marry? His stomach roiled at that thought.

He opened his eyes and gulped part of his coffee, almost choking on the heated liquid.

He had to take one careful step at a time. Right now Marissa was under his care, and without delving into his battered psyche, he knew he wasn't willing to share her with anyone. He'd get her used to him and then he'd see what shots he would call next. By that time she'd have to go along with his decisions, whatever they were.

After all, hadn't she all but admitted that she had been carried away by her own emotions? So he must have had *some* effect on her, whether she refused to voice it or not!

Smugly satisfied with his decision, he leaned back once again and closed his eyes. Visions of a small, dark-haired sprite danced in his dreams.

MARISSA STOOD at the front door and glanced around the apartment once more, her list in her hands. The mover was right about one thing: plants would help. And a few other items she had in mind that were within reach of her pocketbook wouldn't hurt either.

She closed the door and walked swiftly toward the elevator, waving at the small camera on the wall as she walked past, acknowledging that downstairs there was a guard watching her movements. Adam was waiting in the restaurant for her.

Yesterday afternoon and evening had been spent getting her belongings in order and finding where the men had put the smaller items so she could organize them. It turned out to be a wasted effort. They had even stowed her underwear in the proper drawer. The only rearranging she did was in her kitchen cupboards. The men were obviously taller than five foot and had the reach of long-armed gorillas.

The elevator carried her swiftly and silently toward the restaurant floor and she couldn't help the smile that still teased her mouth. It had been there ever since

Adam left yesterday afternoon. He was living up to her first impression that he was overbearing, take-charge and vulnerable. She'd have to be careful not to hurt his feelings while she was busy getting her own way. But the man had to learn from someone that women weren't frail and empty-headed. It might as well be an earth-sciences teacher who taught him that small fact. The elevator opened and she walked toward the double glass doors of the restaurant.

Adam sat at a table for two by one of the large bay windows overlooking the front boulevard. His dark head was bent over a file and he was sipping at a cup of coffee. A frown creased his forehead and she wondered what could cause him such worry until she remembered just how deeply involved he was in so many businesses and chided herself for her naiveté.

"Hi," she said, standing next to the table.

His head flew up and his eyes locked with hers, sending her stomach into a nosedive. No matter what, he was the sexiest man she had ever met.

"Hi, yourself." He smiled slowly, gesturing toward the other chair. "How are you feeling this morning?"

"Fine."

"No upset stomach?"

She reached for her napkin and nodded at the waiter, who had seemingly come from nowhere to motion toward her cup. "The usual morning sickness, but I woke up at six and two hours is enough time to get over it."

He sighed in exasperation. "That's silly. Why don't you get something from your doctor so you won't have to go through this illness."

"It's not illness. It's a baby. And my doctor knows I don't take drugs unless I absolutely need them."

"Okay, okay," he soothed, seeing that stubborn tilt to her chin that presaged a no-win argument. "But order something substantial for breakfast so I'll know you've made the right decision."

After ordering, she sat back and relaxed, watching him fiddle with the papers in front of him. "What's that?"

He glanced at her, then back down again. "My attorney had them delivered this morning," he began casually, by way of explanation. "It's an agreement between you and me. One that we both sign." Her brows rose. "Concerning the baby."

He held the file out to her and she reluctantly took it, glancing quickly at the legal form. Now it was her turn to frown. "You don't think I'll keep my part of our bargain?" she finally asked.

He shook his head. "That's not what it means. It's to ensure that both of us keep to our bargain. It also tells us what is expected."

"I asked for five thousand, this says fifteen. It also says I own the condo free and clear of debt and that you have unlimited visitation rights." Her chin tilted again. "This wasn't our agreement."

"It is now," he stated flatly. "We never had an agreement before. You asked for help and this is what I want in return."

She ignored him. "I won't sign this."

"Yes, you will."

"Why?"

"Because it's my child, too."

Tears glimmered in the corners of her eyes but resentment glittered even brighter. "I wouldn't deny that. But 'unlimited visitation' means that you can disrupt the child's routine on a whim, and I can't tolerate that."

He muttered something under his breath. "Look," he said, exasperation lacing his voice. This was now the get-the-naive-girl-to-be-reasonable routine, and his tone set her teeth on edge. "The agreement is fair to both of us, but if you want to, hire an attorney to look it over. He'll find it to be in order, I'm sure."

Her spine was rigid. "I don't care. I won't own the condo. You won't have unlimited visitation rights." She crossed her arms. "In fact, I'd disappear before I signed something like this. It gives me no control over my own child."

"You came to me!" he whispered forcefully. "You were shaking in your boots and ready to agree to anything I said just two days ago!"

She leaned forward and hissed, "I was not! I was scared of the future and asked your help! Period! Anyone in the same situation would be frightened, but that *never* meant I was spineless!"

"You're impossible!"

"You're overbearing!"

"Your breakfast," the waiter said, staring at each of them, a laden tray in his hands.

Marissa sat back, allowing him access to the place setting in front of her, but her eyes spoke volumes to the man across the table who was also communicating silently.

Their anger seemed to evaporate with the waiter, but stubbornness was clearly etched on Adam's face. Marissa was sure he could see her own stand in her expression. "You were asked to help, not to take over. If you can't help without taking over, then I suggest we call this . . . this arrangement to a halt. Right now."

His face turned to stone. "I'll take you to court."

"You'd have to find me first."

His lips tightened. "I'll find you."

A dark shiver raced down her spine. "No, you won't." She picked up her fork and began to pick at the scrambled eggs in front of her. She was going to need all the strength she had. . . .

"What would it take for a compromise?"

Her eyes darted to his and saw the tinge of defeat there. Just a tinge, for Adam wasn't the kind to give in entirely. "You can keep the condo and request visitation rights as any divorced father would. Weekends and holidays and summer."

"And child support?" He was getting aggressive again.

She sighed, setting down her fork. "Only if it is reasonable. You won't own either of us, nor will you be allowed to spoil the baby by giving her things that she doesn't need or want."

"He."

"What?"

"The baby's a boy."

"No, it isn't."

His grin was infectious. "We can't seem to agree on anything, can we?"

"At least you believe that the baby's yours," she said, and his hand covered hers, giving it a light squeeze.

"Maybe it's a basis to build this new relationship on," he suggested, his voice husky and oddly humble. He was as confused about the best way to handle this situation as she was!

She smiled, squeezing his hand in turn. "Maybe," she hedged, unwilling to commit further than that.

"More coffee?" The waiter appeared once more, the glass pot in his hand poised over Marissa's cup.

"Yes," they both said, then grinned at each other again.

By the time Marissa slipped inside the dark confines of her car and drove out of the underground parking lot, she was humming.

Adam might be a strong-willed man, but he was fair and just. She merely had to stay on top of the situation so that he couldn't gain control of her life or that of her baby.

Regret—deep and well rooted—filled her with an underlying sadness. She couldn't shake the feeling, so chose to ignore it. After thinking she loved him for the past three years, she now knew it, but was as helpless to do anything about it as she had been before.

If only... She refused to dwell on impossible dreams, instead turning her thoughts to shopping.

A large nursery was going out of business and the plants she needed were less than half-price. A small discount house had darling scatter rugs of all sizes on sale, and she chose two from the myriad patterns. One was in creams and blues that would look perfect between the couch and the fireplace, while the other in peaches and blues would grace the tiled floor of the entryway.

With the car loaded, she drove back to the apartment, tired but satisfied. She'd take a short nap and afterward make arrangements to have her phone connected, then see to the details of terminating the lease on her apartment and transferring her mail. There was still so much to do.

ALONE, ADAM LINGERED over one more cup of coffee as he stared out the restaurant window. There was still a rueful smile inside him wanting to bloom, but he refused to allow it. He was irritated with himself. He had allowed her to wind him around her little finger and he'd just sat there like an idiot! A grinning idiot!

His smile kept pushing for release.

How had he managed to ignore her for three years? He knew she was beautiful and smart, and that should have drawn him to her to begin with. Had he also instinctively known that she had a stubborn streak as wide as the Mississippi River and twice as deep? A challenge if ever there was one.

He sipped at the hot brew. *Face it, Adam Pierce. She's the first woman to enter your life and confuse you with behavior you'd only seen in dealing with businessmen.* All right, so he was a male chauvinist. But most women were drawn to him because of his money or position, and if they said otherwise, he never trusted them.

But Marissa was different. She originally came to him out of compassion. She had felt sorry for him, he was sure, and sensed that he was lower than he had ever been. When he'd needed solace, she had given him herself. And then she'd returned to him because she needed monetary help.

He didn't feel sorry for her. He felt protective of her, hassled because she wouldn't do as he thought best, and frustrated because he still wanted her. But most of all, he was confused because she wasn't following the pattern of the other women he had known.

And when she was around, he felt contented....

The waiter appeared, plugging in the small phone and handing it to him. "Your attorney, sir. He says he must speak to you."

"Thank you," he muttered before turning to the machine that was demanding his attention. "What's up Mike?"

"Did you get the papers signed?"

"Not yet."

Mike's laugh echoed through the wires. "I didn't think so. You pushed too hard too soon."

"I don't need an I-told-you-so right now."

"You never need one, but in this instance I'm saying it anyway."

Adam sighed. "Enough." He glared at the offending papers sitting on the edge of the table. "If you have anything else to say, say it now. I'm running late."

"You've got to finish up the papers on the new restaurant at the top of the tower. They've called twice this morning to check on it."

"Tell them to eliminate the biyearly check on the books and I'll agree to it. Not until then."

"And you think Marissa's stubborn?"

He heard the teasing in Mike's voice and knew he was right, but stood his ground. "If they don't give me an annual report to get their percentage, the deal's off. Tell them that for me."

"Gotcha."

"Good. Talk to you later."

"Right. And, Adam? Go easy on her. I think you've finally met your match."

"You haven't even met her."

"No, but everyone's talking about the effect she's had on you in the past two days. It's about time someone shook up your little world."

"Thanks, friend," Adam said dryly. "I've got problems, and you're right there, pushing me down."

Mike's chuckle echoed in the receiver before the connection was severed with a click.

4

BY THE TIME Marissa made it back to her apartment and deposited all the packages and plants in the middle of the floor she was exhausted. She had bypassed the eagle-eyed guards by going directly from the garage to the apartment, and now she was regretting her streak of independence—short-lived as it was. Carrying a baby was far more tiring than she had ever dreamed possible. Not that there was any doubt about continuing on her chosen path no matter how arduous. She wrapped her arms around her stomach protectively and smiled. There was never any doubt.

Without bothering to do anything else but complete a yawn, she headed for her bedroom to take a much-needed nap, her eyes drifting closed almost immediately. With a deep sigh, she turned on her side and curled into a ball, letting slumber overtake her tired mind and body.

It was twilight when she awakened, groggy but more able to complete the tasks she had set for herself. She glanced out the large windows that offered a golden-glistening view of the almost all-glass Houston skyline, then turned away to set herself about the next task. Above all else, she had to keep busy. When she was busy she didn't have time to think.

The assortment of plants set in strategic places and the muted colors of the complementary rugs made all the difference in the world. Instead of the living room looking big and empty, it seemed spacious but cozy, the new additions cutting the large room into smaller conversation areas.

She was admiring her handiwork when she spotted the telephone on the small table by the fireplace. As if it were alive, she stepped toward the instrument and carefully lifted the receiver. A dial tone buzzed in her ear. Holding it away from her, she stared at it again. She hadn't had a chance to order service yet! How... Amazement gave way to anger. With fingers that were rigid, she punched out Adam's office number. Tapping her foot, she listened to the rings. After fifteen of them—she counted—she gave up. But later...she'd take care of it later.

She began again, calling information to ask for her own number. "I'm sorry, but there is no number for that name," the operator intoned.

"There has to be. I'm in my own apartment and this is my phone."

"Then please call the business office between nine and five and they will handle it."

She hung up the phone, still fuming. Oh, it'd be handled all right! But not by the office.

She practically goose-stepped into the kitchen to begin dinner, her anger so forceful it propelled her into action. When less than fifteen minutes later her phone rang, she froze until she realized who it had to be.

Adam.

No one else could get her number, including herself!

"Hello?" she answered in a bad imitation of a German accent.

There was a moment of silence. Then Adam's voice demanded an answer. "Marissa."

"Not here. She go on trip." Her voice was high-pitched and strained with the accent.

"Then tell her that I'll be there within the next hour and I want her to have dinner with me...."

"She gone. She have no phone."

"...and that her new phone number is written on the underside of the phone."

"Not her phone. Bossman's phone. She no have phone!"

His next words told her that his patience was at an end. "Dammit, Marissa! Stop playing childish games!"

But her anger was stronger than his impatience. "Then, dammit, Adam! Stop treating me like a child! If I want a phone, I'll get one! And not one that isn't even listed under my own name!"

"I did that to protect you."

"From what? The bogeyman?"

"I thought you'd be pleased."

"Pleased?" Her voice squeaked with anger. "Pleased that I now look as if you're paying for me? That I'm some kind of property that can be bought and sold? That I'm too dim-witted to take care of myself?"

"You're pregnant and tired," he offered patronizingly.

His tone was just what she needed to whip her fury into a froth. "Does pregnancy guarantee that all my brains fell out?"

"Sometimes it's hard to tell." His voice dripped with as much sarcasm as hers.

She took a deep breath, willing herself to calm down enough to answer coherently. "Go soak your head in the nearest commode, Adam Pierce," she said in a quietly firm voice, then hung up the phone with shaking fingers.

One glass of wine only, on occasion, was what the doctor had told her, and she never needed it more than now. She stood on the balcony and let the heat envelop her chilled body and pretended that tears didn't want to fall. One hand covered her still-flat stomach as if giving the baby a hug.

This, too, would pass. Somehow.

She ignored the doorbell when it rang. Since this crazy weekend had begun she hadn't had a chance to tell her friends where she was, so the person on the other side of the door was the one person she didn't want to talk to: Adam Pierce.

The doorbell peeled again. She took a sip of her wine, willing her body to relax instead of winding up like a too-tight spring.

The doorbell sounded again.

She forced her eyes to focus on the expressway below, the cars rushing like ants on the way back to their colonies.

There was no noise, but all her senses were tuned to the room behind her. She whirled around, anger flashing in her eyes and straightening her stance as she spotted Adam standing by the patio doors, an enormous bouquet of pink-tinged roses in his arms. He looked almost humble. Almost.

She couldn't help the smile that tugged at her mouth, but she refused to say the first word. Silence stretched like a rubber band between them.

Adam sighed, running a hand through his hair. "I'm big enough to know when to say I'm sorry. I probably shouldn't have done anything to help without consulting you."

"Even your apology is a roundabout tribute to your virtues," she said, unable to stop herself from pointing that out.

"I'm trying." His arrogance returned with the raising of a brow.

"I know," she said so softly it was almost a whisper, and his eyes fastened on her mouth as she formed the words. Taking a few steps toward him she stared up at his face. It was lined with fatigue, but there was also tenderness there that filled her with a quiet joy. "Are those for me?"

He smiled ruefully and the lines of his face changed dramatically. "Only if you don't throw them back at me."

"I promise," she said solemnly, taking them in her own arms and burying her nose in the bouquet so she could breathe the delicate scent. The petals were as soft as a newborn baby's skin.

He touched the side of her neck, his thumb caressing the tender skin just behind her ear. "I didn't mean to upset you." His voice was husky, sending ripples of excitement down her back.

"I know. You thought you were doing me a favor by taking over my life."

"I did."

Her brow furrowed as she tried to prove her own sincerity. "But I *like* doing things for myself, Adam. I like making my own decisions, deciding my own future."

His finger toyed with an curl. "I know it took a while, but I think you've convinced me."

She reached up on tiptoe and grazed his cheek with a whisper-soft kiss. "Pax?" she whispered.

"Peace," he answered, his voice as soft as hers. The sincerity of his tone soothed her right down to her toes, but his touch set her nerve endings on fire. She was immobile—afraid to move and lose the contact of his flesh, but even more afraid to remain so breathlessly close to him in case he took her actions as a blatant invitation to repeat the scene that had brought them together.

He bent his head and brushed his lips against hers, teasing them with his warmth. Her breath caught in her throat and her eyes widened before half closing in a slumberous way.

A groan rumbled from him as he wrapped his arms around her and pulled her close against his own body. The roses were trapped between them, crushed.

His mouth was rough with the need that overwhelmed him, his fears that she would disappear into a puff of air more intense because he needed her so much. So very much. Her body was warm and pliant, her softness molded to his hardness.

He trembled, a shiver shooting throughout his body, and he clamped his arms tighter around her. His tongue foraged the sweetness of her parted mouth, restrained urgency apparent in every intimate movement. Another groan echoed through him as she tentatively responded with her own timid thrusts.

Her hands encircled his neck, nails scraping against his hairline to elicit another, even deeper reaction. He was almost out of control with desire and couldn't seem to pull himself back to sanity.

He had to seek, to touch, to feel secure in her arms. He trembled again as his palm fit cozily around the softness of her breast.

But her voice stilled his questing fingers. "No," she whispered, her hand covering his.

With great effort he opened his eyes. His breathing was so shallow, his heartbeat so erratic, that he could hardly focus his gaze on her resolute face.

They both stilled, standing frozen in time, in space.

"No," she said again, but this time mixed with firmness there was regret.

He rested his forehead on the top of her head as he fought for control. A control he had never before lost in all his thirty-odd years. It seemed as if they stood that way forever, but his inner clock told him it was only minutes.

Stepping away, he ran a shaking hand through his hair. "I'm sorry," he growled, still attempting to gain control and kicking himself for losing it. "It won't happen again."

She touched his cheek with her palm, cradling his jaw. "It was both our faults. It just got out of hand." He could feel her fingers trembling. Was she frightened? Was she as moved by his touch as he was by hers? He couldn't tell.

She stepped away from him, walking with sweet, dainty steps toward the kitchen, cradling the crushed roses against her shoulder as if they were a baby needing burping.

That thought washed over him like a thousand ice cubes.

Water splashed in the kitchen sink, reinforcing the chill sweeping through his veins. He turned and strode toward the door, the fear of confronting his own emotions forcing him to run from that which he wanted most: Marissa.

Just as she turned off the faucet, Marissa heard the click of the front door closing. Her heart sank to her toes. Adam had left.

She should have known. She said no and he walked. He hadn't changed his mind or his feelings about her. His words when she had confronted him in the shopping mall now haunted the recesses of her mind. You were available.

He was right, she had been available to him. But her reasons for going to bed with him were entirely different and had nothing to do with availability.

But how was he to know? Certainly not by her behavior, now or in the past! Perhaps he thought that because she'd gone to bed with him once, she should be willing to do so again? After all, the harm was already done. She was pregnant and nothing worse could happen.

She reached for an empty jelly jar and began arranging the flowers, concentrating on that task so the tears that wanted to flow wouldn't.

All she could do was stay out of his way. No, that wasn't quite right. All she could do was not invite sexual advances. *Keep it business. Keep it friendly.* Yes, that was it. But she knew the decision was easier made than kept.

ADAM HEADED straight for the bar in his apartment. This wasn't the best time to drink, but he sure as hell couldn't think of a reason not too, either.

After pouring a glass of Scotch, he clutched it in his hand and plopped down on the couch. The day was bright and beautiful and the glass and chrome buildings of the skyline seemed to be lit from inside.

He had just made an absolute fool of himself. And for the first time in his life, he didn't know what to do about it.

He'd apologized, his conscience told him, but he knew it wasn't enough. Words were cheap. It was the action that counted, and he had just done enough to get himself in hot water with Marissa.

But what scared him the most was that he had totally lost control of himself. He had *never* done that before! Even when he was young and thought he was in love he hadn't felt that overwhelming need he'd just experienced with Marissa. In fact, he had prided himself on never allowing any woman enough access to his emotions that he would miss her when she left. Or he left.

This whole situation was out of control. With his free hand he clutched his knee and squeezed, bringing himself back to his own apartment. He wouldn't allow himself to drift back into the memory of being in Marissa's arms.

From somewhere down deep, he recognized the problem. It was the baby. He wanted it and all it represented: home, love, family, peace, contentment, laughter. And never being lonely again. Funny, but he hadn't even realized he *was* lonely until Marissa had moved into his life and he had known the feeling of being *with* someone, even when she wasn't there.

"Damn her!" he muttered to himself, and his voice echoed through the room. She had upset his routine, his emotions, his thoughts—his life. And she had threatened to leave his protection if he pressed too hard. He couldn't let that happen.

He suddenly wanted her with a passion that bordered on obsession. He wanted her in his arms, his heart, his power. But it was very obvious that the woman didn't share his goals.

Setting his untouched drink on the coffee table, he reached for the phone and punched the numbers quickly. "Judi? Get me a flight to Dallas sometime tonight. Then set up a meeting with Harrigan for tomorrow morning. We'll get this leasing business over with this week."

With a terse goodbye, he set the phone down and strode toward the bedroom, his drink forgotten in the flurry of movement that would momentarily erase his problems.

His bags were packed in record time. After one more call to confirm his secretary's arrangements, he was out the door.

Stopping at the front desk, he scribbled a note, tucked it into an envelope, sealed it and placed it on the security counter. "Please give this to Marissa Madison, Arthur," he said over his shoulder as he stalked to the elevator.

"Yes, sir," the young man answered, but he was talking to electronically closing doors.

Adam realized he'd bought himself some time to think. He had three days to pull his act together before he confronted Marissa again. Three long days . . .

"BUT HE DOESN'T seem to have a very good opinion of women in general." Marissa leaned her head against the couch. She was sitting on the floor, knees bent, in her favorite at-home uniform: an old sweatshirt that exclaimed *Corona* and a pair of faded cutoffs. She held a steaming cup of tea in both hands.

"Have you asked him why?" prodded Becca, her friend and fellow teacher. "I mean, how many bad moments could a hunk like that have? Or is that the problem? Could it be that every woman falls all over herself to get to him and he's used to having his choice?" Becca's light brown hair glinted in the late-afternoon light as she leaned forward to emphasize her point. She was sitting in the same position as Marissa, only she used as her back prop the small upholstered secondhand chair Marissa had bought that afternoon. Her brown eyes darted around the room appreciatively. "Especially with his money."

Marissa straightened her legs and stared hard at her sneaker-clad toes. "I think that's the problem. He thinks everyone is after his money—especially women. And he also thinks that all he has to do to make women happy is dole out greenbacks like ornaments for a Christmas tree. When the tree is filled, the girl should be thrilled to death. It doesn't matter that the tree is fake or the Christmas spirit is missing."

Becca grinned. "Ever the philosopher," she teased, but her smile faded as she asked her next question. "Have you told your parents yet?"

Marissa stared into her cup remembering her mother's worried tone of voice. There hadn't been one reprimand, although Marissa certainly deserved it. And that made her feel even more guilty about her behavior. Instead of trusting her own love and instincts when it came to Adam, she should have looked a little deeper into *his* motives.... "I spoke to them this afternoon—right after I called you."

"How's your mom taking it?"

"She's coming for a visit in two weeks. My stepfather has business in town, and she's coming with him."

"Was she hurt?"

Marissa nodded, her brown eyes bright with the unshed tears that seemed to plague her lately. "But she'll stand by my decision, no matter what." She swallowed hard. "My stepdad, Garner, said the same thing."

"Wow! My mother would be delivering kittens by now!" Becca exclaimed before she realized what she had said. She reached out her hand and patted Marissa on the leg. "Sorry."

A chuckle erupted from Marissa. "If I was having kittens, this whole situation might be easier. At least they grow quickly and start out on their own at a young age."

"Are you really keeping the baby, 'Rissa? Won't that be difficult for you? I mean . . ." She halted, unable to express her curiosity tactfully and embarrassed to go on.

"I'm keeping it. Period." Marissa's eyes narrowed determinedly. "And it won't be too hard. Especially if Adam Pierce has his way."

"He's going to continue to help?" Becca sat up straighter at this juicy piece of information.

"I received a note from him, telling me that he's out of town for the rest of the week, and then his attorney sent over a new contract for me to sign."

"And?"

"And he wants limited visitation rights, in return for which he will pay child support in the sum of one thousand dollars a month."

Becca's big eyes grew even bigger. "A thousand a month? Twelve thousand a year?" Her voice nearly cracked.

Marissa nodded. "And the unlimited use of this condo."

Becca's mouth dropped open. "*This* condo?"

"*This* condo."

"That's fabulous!"

"No, it's blackmail. I can't stay here and expect to get a job in this school district. Everybody knows me, knows that I'm not married. Otherwise I would have signed the contract for this fall. As it is right now, no school board will hire a teacher who isn't a perfect example for their students. I have to wait until the baby is born and pretend I was married and divorced."

Becca slumped. "No. You're right. You wouldn't be able to teach under these circumstances—" she grinned and Marissa could almost see the light bulb over her head "—unless you went to another district. Bellaire, maybe. Or Sharpstown. Neither one of them are too far away by car."

"Maybe." Marissa didn't sound hopeful and she knew it, but chances were slim to none for her career. "I couldn't get a job this fall, anyway. They won't take a chance that I can't finish out the semester." She shook off the feeling of helplessness that had hounded her since she found she was pregnant. Right now, the only important thing was the baby.

Her baby.

She pictured an infant that smelled like talcum powder, with ebony curls and eyes that were wide and bright gray. With a small dimple in her pudgy chin and dark, winged brows that would furrow together when she was angry. Like Adam.

It would be a girl. She just knew it. Cuddly. Sweet. Someone to receive all her love without reservation.

"Marissa?"

"Hmm?" Her eyes were lightly clouded with fluffy dreams.

"Is there anything I can do to help? I mean, you can always move in with me if you feel the need. Adam sounds like a dream, but I don't want you to think you've got nowhere else to go."

Becca's sincerity touched her as nothing else had in the past five crazy days. She reached for her friend's hand, giving a squeeze. "Thanks. I'll remember that," she promised softly.

Becca nodded.

They both leaned back and enjoyed the silence that only friends could share. The golden afternoon sun turned to dusk and shadows etched themselves on the skyline. Her patio became coolly shaded.

Even though she was inside, she shivered. Her thoughts had been so caught up with Adam that she had to shake herself to quit the what-if game she'd been playing. What if Adam had loved her as she loved him? What if . . .

"Would you like to stay for dinner?" she asked Becca brightly, determined to shake off the depression that had cloyingly wrapped itself around her shoulders.

"No, thanks," her friend said reluctantly as she slowly stood and stretched. "I'm supposed to meet some friends for pizza and if I don't get going, I'll be late." She grinned. "Everyone always says I'm never on time, but I promised myself that I'd surprise them tonight."

"Shock would best describe their reaction if you're punctual," Marissa teased, getting to her feet.

"Say, why don't you join us? You know half the crowd already—Ted, Mary, Pete and Joanne, along with a few others." At Marissa's expression, Becca pleaded. "Why not? You'd only be sitting around here by yourself all night, getting lonely and ugly."

"Thanks." Marissa grinned in spite of herself. Becca's enthusiasm for life was contagious. She was a talented teacher possessing the one attribute Marissa loved best: unfailing loyalty. "Can you wait until I change?" she asked, glancing at her cutoffs.

"You bet, but hurry. I'm determined to be early!"

Marissa ran to throw on a pair of jeans and a big, bulky sweater. Anything, including questions from curious acquaintances, was better than feeling sorry for herself in a big empty apartment. Her mind was already too occupied with what Adam was doing right now. But she couldn't help pricking herself by wondering if he was alone....

ADAM SAT across from Jeff Harrigan in the hotel bar and wondered what in the hell he was doing in Dallas. He had met with Jeff early that morning and they had gone over their mutual business until there was nothing left to discuss, unless they talked about what was uppermost in Adam's mind: Marissa. It shocked him that that was exactly what he wanted to do. Not one to disclose his personal life before, he now realized that he needed a sounding board for his muddled emotions.

"Are you going to take her up on her offer?" Jeff asked, and Adam glanced up, a frown creasing his forehead.

"What?"

"That girl sitting across from us." Jeff nodded his head sideways toward the next table. "She keeps giving you the eye. Are you playing hard to get, or are you just not interested?"

"Not interested," Adam said, glancing at the blond woman who was more than obviously endowed. Bored, he stared back down at the bowl of peanut mix in front of him. "Take her up on her offer if you want to."

"Thanks," Jeff drawled. An East Texas boy born and bred, he slowed his speech so much that at times Adam wanted to help him form the words. "But if you're not interested, why should I be?"

Adam chuckled. "No challenge?"

"Nope." Jeff leaned back, tilting his head so he could look down his well-formed nose in his most intimidating manner. "What's up, Adam? You've been in a blue funk most of the day. If I didn't know better I'd say that you had something on your mind besides business."

"Like what?" Adam took a sip of his Jack Daniel's and water, stalling the conversation he knew was coming.

"Women."

"Woman," Adam corrected with a sigh.

Jeff nodded and raised his own glass.

"The mother of my child."

The glass stilled in the air, Jeff's eyes widening in disbelief. "You're married and you never told me?" he asked incredulously. "We've been friends for a long time, dude, and even though we don't see each other very often, I never thought you'd do something that drastic without letting me know."

"We're not married." Adam tested that phrase and found that it bothered him. Why? Wasn't that what he had accused her of trying to do: getting him hog-tied for life?

"And she's going to have your baby?"

Adam nodded. "In December, just before the New Year."

Jeff's glass returned to the table slowly as he continued to stare at his friend. "Do you want it? Does she?"

"It's my baby. I want it." There was a determined edge in his voice. For the first time since he had seen Marissa last week, he admitted just how much the baby meant to him.

Jeff leaned forward but his face held the expression of innocence he used when he was being cagey. "And what does the mother want?"

"She wants the baby, but not particularly the father," Adam stated, taking another sip of his drink. Damn that woman! What was wrong with him? Most women would fight tooth and nail for what he had to offer, but Marissa threw him back in the sea of unmarrieds before he had even proposed to her! He flashed back to yesterday afternoon and the kiss they had shared. He was still astounded by his reaction. And her own emotions hadn't been that hard to read, either. She had wanted him, he was sure. The blatant tenderness that had warmed her eyes and filtered from her touch to his senses wouldn't have been there if she hadn't.

"What do you want?" Jeff asked.

"I want my child."

"And the mother?"

Adam grinned ruefully. The joke was on him. "I want the mother, too, but she's a handful—stubborn, temperamental and a female chauvinist."

Jeff's laugh told him what his friend was going to say before he said it. "Just what the doctor ordered. Someone to teach you the facts of life."

"Like hell," he gritted.

"I'd love to meet her."

"You won't. She doesn't want a thing to do with me. She won't even sign the child-support contract, for chrissake!"

"Contract?" The smile was wiped off Jeff's face.

Adam nodded. "Mike wrote out a contract stating that I'd pay generous child support and give her a few extras in exchange for a few minor points."

"Such as?"

"Unlimited visitation."

"And she wouldn't bite?"

He shook his head.

"She must be some little lady," Jeff said softly. He was obviously awed that Marissa wouldn't sell out. "My friend, I think you've met your match."

"No kidding." There wasn't any joy in Adam's voice. He wasn't even sure he could meet the challenge. He finished his drink and set the glass on the table. Sitting in a bar in Dallas wasn't going to solve his problems, but working it out with Marissa would. "I've got to go," he said, standing up. "If you need me to finish up this deal, grab me at the office tomorrow."

Jeff stood and held out his hand, a wide grin on his handsome face. "Will do. And good luck, Adam."

"Thanks," he said before walking out and heading toward the lobby phones. He'd call Marissa and ask her to meet him for breakfast in the morning. Perhaps they could solve one problem at a time.

But the phone rang unanswered. Adam glanced at his watch. It was after ten. Where in the hell was she? Was she ill? Out with another man? His temper threatened to explode as he thought of all the things she could be doing without him.

It was definitely time to go home and take care of business . . . Marissa business.

5

MARISSA LET HERSELF into her apartment without bothering to turn on the lights. Even though it was well past midnight, the skyline was ablaze and its incandescence flowed through the large patio doors to softly illuminate her living room.

With a heavy sigh she dropped her purse on the floor, curled up in the corner of her small couch and stared out at the shadowy view. She'd tried so hard to have a good time tonight. But even surrounded by friends, she had never felt so alone....

"Staying out until all hours of the night isn't good for the baby."

Her heart stopped as she jumped at the sound of Adam's voice. Reaching quickly, she flicked on the lamp. "Scaring me to death doesn't help, either," she said, her eyes narrowing as she took in the tired lines that creased his handsome face.

He stood next to the window, leaning against the wall, his arms and ankles crossed. Only his darkened eyes gave away his anger. "Where in the hell were you?"

"Out with friends. Where the hell were you?"

"Don't cuss." He pulled away from the wall and jammed his hands in the pockets of his jeans. "I left you a note. I had to go to Dallas on business."

"For three days, I think it said. Forgive me if I'm wrong, but didn't you leave just yesterday?"

"I finished early. When I couldn't get a hold of you I got worried."

She raised her brows. "You mean you thought I was mugged in the lobby or garage with the guards watching? Or in the elevator and hallways with the all-seeing cameras?"

He ignored her sarcasm. "Who were you with?"

"I told you—friends."

"What kind of friends? Male? Female?"

"Both," she snapped, her patience at an end. Did he think he owned her just because he paid her rent?

"Are you looking for an alternative to my care and support?"

Anger washed over her. She stood and faced him, her body stiff with indignation. With great effort she kept her hands clenched at her sides, nails biting into her palms. "No, but *they* claim to be my friends, which is a whole lot more than you can declare."

He stepped closer to her, his hands leaving his pockets to rest on her shoulders. Surprisingly, his touch was soft and his look regretful. "I'm sorry. I've been a bastard ever since you met me, haven't I?"

Unable to speak past the lump in her throat, she nodded.

A small grimace tightened his mouth. "I wish I had an explanation for my behavior, but to tell you the truth, I don't. All I can do is say I'm sorry."

Her eyes searched his, fear and hope mingling inside her. Finally she spoke. "I accept your apology," she said quietly.

His hands tightened, then stroked her flesh beneath the sweater. "Thanks."

They stared at each other a moment, neither sure what to do next. Marissa cleared her throat. "Would you like a cup of decaf coffee?"

He shook his head. "No, but can we just sit together quietly for a little while? Then I'll leave and you can get your beauty sleep. I promise."

His lack of arrogance surprised her. It also frightened her. What had happened to him since she had seen him last? She turned from the magnetic heat of him and reluctantly returned to her perch on the couch, then spoke coldly, "And when you leave, would you also leave your key on the table?"

His sigh of defeat ran down to her toes as he took the seat next to her. "All right. It's only fair. I just wanted to check on you—make sure you were all right."

"I appreciate your concern, but I'm really capable of taking care of myself. Honest." On impulse, she placed her hand on his knee, underlining with her touch the sincerity of her words.

At his indrawn breath she snapped her hand away. "No, don't," he said hoarsely, clasping her hand and replacing it on his thigh. "I like your touch," he admitted softly. His arm came around and pulled her to the side of him, fitting her curves to him as if they had been made for each other. "Relax," he whispered in her ear. "I won't bite. I just want to hold you for a while."

The stiffness ebbed slowly from her body as she sank against him, stifling a yawn with her hand. The apartment was quiet. Serene. His touch was soothing, making her feel pampered. . . .

"Was your trip successful?" she asked in a sleepy voice.

"Yes." His hand rubbed against her rhythmically, lulling her further into drowsiness. "Did you have a nice evening?"

"Umm," she said, moving her head against his chest as if to find a softer place. "I met some teachers at a pizza parlor and we talked ourselves silly."

"Sounds like fun."

The thought that he sounded wistful was dismissed. He had everything, so how could he envy a group of broke teachers? "It was. They're a great bunch, and all dedicated even when the odds are against them." Her eyes closed, opened, then drifted closed again. He was so comfortable. . . . One more sigh and she was asleep.

ADAM SAT on the small couch in the dark, reluctant to give up his hold on Marissa even while she slept. Her head was nestled against his shoulder, the mahogany curls scattered across his chest. He swallowed hard, attempting to keep the lump in his throat at bay. She was safe. She was here. That's all that mattered.

He had rushed to the Dallas airport and taken the next flight out, arriving in Houston in less than an hour. But the time he'd endured here, waiting for her to return, had seemed an eternity. He had imagined all sorts of things, none of them flattering to her, even though he knew better.

He knew what was happening to him, but he was powerless to stop it.

He was falling in love with Marissa, and the pain was overwhelming. Especially when he knew that his past behavior was reprehensible and might cost him her friendship, her trust . . . and her love.

She sighed and wiggled closer and his arm tightened. She was so tiny, so soft. And such a fighter! His other hand came down and gently touched the slight mound of her stomach.

His baby. Their baby. A miracle in his palm. A miracle he wanted so badly he could taste it. But he wanted both of them—a package deal.

He almost groaned at his choice of words. How many package deals had he put together in his life? Fifty? A hundred? Hundreds? Yet this one counted the most. In fact, his whole future depended on this one.

Despite a few setbacks, he'd always been good in business, but he only now realized how little he knew about personal relationships and how they were supposed to work. He'd never had a living example.

Somehow he would have to convince Marissa to stay with him. He would have to prove his reliability in terms of being the father and provider she needed emotionally. Obviously his financial reliability wasn't an issue. Having her in his home and heart was his only hope for peace of mind.

"Adam?" Her sleepy voice broke into his reverie.

"What, honey?" he murmured, his lips moving against the top of her head.

"You should be in bed. You've got to be exhausted." Her voice sounded three octaves lower than usual—almost a lover's whisper.

He chuckled huskily, his heart pounding heavily. "I didn't want to leave such a tempting bundle alone."

She leaned back and attempted to focus her sleepy eyes on him. "Go on so I can get some sleep."

He dropped his arms reluctantly and stood towering over her. Then, as if pulled by a magnetic force, he leaned down and gave her a chaste kiss on the forehead. "I'll see you in the morning."

She smiled. "Right."

"Good night, tiger," he whispered, but she didn't hear him. She had already curled up on the couch and allowed sleep to overpower her again.

He stared at her a moment, then slipped into her room and pulled the peach-colored comforter from her bed. He returned to the couch and with careful movements, he covered her, gently tucking the fabric around her neck and chin.

One more kiss, then very softly he opened the door and let himself out. As he walked down the hall he hummed an old romantic ballad. His fingers were curled around Marissa's key.

WHEN MARISSA AWOKE, there were no crackers by her bedside. There was no bedside. She forced her eyes to focus, glancing around for a few seconds before she realized where she was. In her new apartment. In her living room. Curled on her small couch that would give a midget cramped muscles.

She lay still and stared at the ceiling as she took inventory of her health. Her head was clearing rapidly— no headache. Her mouth felt as if it needed a good brushing, but there wasn't any of the pinched-as-a-lemon feeling she usually suffered. And her stomach was as calm as pond water.

She closed her eyes and smiled. Adam had been jealous last night. She hadn't expected that. But was his jealousy based on wanting her for himself, or on the fact that she was the mother of his child? She prayed for the former, but her instincts told her it was the latter. For her own peace of mind, she decided she'd better stop those fantasies.

Yet, he'd held her half the night, his arms cradling her as if she were a treasure. And his lips had felt warm against her forehead. He liked her, she knew it. He just didn't love her.

But it was a start. Perhaps if they could just learn to trust each other, they'd become friends. If her parents had ever been friends, her own childhood wouldn't have been so hard. Instead, her mother loved and lost, and her father . . . Well, her father had never loved, just resented the intrusion into his life of a young girl and her baby. She'd grown up without a father, and it had been so lonely. She didn't want that for her child.

Her baby had to have the advantages of having parents who, if they couldn't love each other, would at least love their child. That was the most important thing of all.

She had made her choice. She was going to be a single parent for the rest of her life because she just couldn't envision loving anyone except Adam. And that was a futile emotion where he was concerned. The only way their futures would mesh was through friendship.

She'd be as friendly and honest and nice to Adam as she could. She'd try not to rock his boat, and maybe he'd see that she would uphold her promise not to interfere in his life. Maybe he'd even learn to love his child. They'd become good friends, with a common bond of love....

Her stomach roiled and she stood on shaky legs. The baby was waking up and she didn't have her crackers.

ADAM STOOD in front of the mirror and adjusted his tie once more. Early that afternoon he'd sent flowers to Marissa and enclosed a card that told her he was picking her up at eight o'clock for dinner, ending the note with *We have unfinished business*, hoping her curiosity would be aroused.

If things went well, he was going to propose tonight, and he was nervous as hell.

After holding her in his arms half the night, he knew he couldn't let her go. He was falling in love hard and fast and his only recourse was action—marriage. Maybe then he could relax and concentrate on business again. But right now she was invading his every thought and it was driving him crazy!

With one more glance at the mirror he strode from the room and over to the door, his steps purposeful. He couldn't wait to see her again. Marissa. His stomach warmed at the very thought of her. She was everything he had never encountered in the women in his life: honest, winsome, impish, delightful.

No matter how much he tried to bribe or intimidate her, she still wouldn't sign his child-support contract because it wasn't good for the baby. *Integrity*—a good word.

Impatiently he punched her doorbell. She never did the expected. What if she refused to go with him tonight? The thought hadn't occurred to him until now, but once born it grew rapidly. By the time he heard the tap of her heels on the tile floor on the other side of the door he was sure she'd refuse his invitation.

"Hi," she said, smiling. The jade-green caftan she wore fell to the floor in soft, seductive folds. Her hair cascaded over her shoulders like a sparkling black waterfall. Wide brown eyes were filled with golden lights of mischief. "Won't you come in?"

"Thanks," he said, stepping into the hallway. He sniffed the air and frowned. Something was cooking. "Didn't you get my note?"

She nodded, still smiling. "But you never called to confirm, and I had already invited guests over for dinner."

"Here?" His frown deepened.

"Of course." She laughed softly. "This is where I live, isn't it?"

"Why didn't you tell me?"

Her eyes widened innocently. "How? I don't have your home phone number and you never called me, remember?"

He'd forgotten, having given her every other number to be able to contact him during the day. He opened his mouth to retort that she could have gotten ahold of him through Kenny at the lobby, but her smile bewitched him. He wasn't sure whether he should turn her over his lap or kiss her until she couldn't breathe. The latter seemed far more tempting. "You could have left a note at the desk," he finally got out.

She turned toward the living room, smiling over her shoulder. "You're right," she conceded. "Come on, I want you to meet my friends."

There was no alternative but to follow. A young dark-haired man in a polo sweater and a pair of well-worn cords lounged in the small upholstered chair next to the patio, a drink dangling from his fingers, his eyes fastened on the darkened skyline.

"Ted? I'd like you to meet Adam Pierce. Ted teaches English at the same high school in which I taught," she said. Ted stood, and both men eyed each other warily as they shook hands.

"Do I hear voices?" Becca's call from the kitchen came seconds before she appeared at the doorway, salad tongs in her hand. Her already big eyes lit up appreciatively when they landed on Adam. He was standing in front of Ted as if to draw blood with the first blow. "You must be Adam," she said, stretching out her hand as she walked toward him. "I'm Becca Hines, another fellow teacher."

Suddenly Adam grinned, almost taking her breath away with the warmth. "I'm very pleased to meet you, Becca Hines. You renew my faith in my own instincts," he teased, noting that Marissa's face had turned a rosy pink. Both women had purposely set him up to believe Ted was wooing Marissa. They were two of a kind. Three could play that game. "And did you work with Marissa, too?"

She nodded. "We even went to college together. Now I see I should have joined a fraternity as a Little Sister instead of wasting my time with a sorority."

"And you tell each other everything. Right?" Grooves deepened Adam's tanned cheeks as he spoke.

Marissa's heart sank as she watched one more woman fall under his spell. Didn't he already have enough of a line formed to bask in his charms? Marissa stepped in front of Adam, blocking Becca's view. "Probably only as much as you tell your good friends." She glanced up at him. "You *do* have good friends, don't you?"

"Do you want me to admit that I do and ruin your image of me as an ogre?" he countered, his hand curving around her arm, then sliding down to capture her hand. "Or admit that I don't so you can pity me?"

"You've never been an ogre. Just arrogant." Her voice had become lower and she forgot for just a moment that there were others in the room. His gray eyes danced with light, mesmerizing her, holding her motionless.

"I'm glad," he said huskily. "Given more time, perhaps I can convince you I'm human."

She tilted her head as if studying him. "Perhaps, but I'd keep my money in my pocket if I were you."

A muscle twitched in his cheek as he tried to hold back a smile. "Not the stuff good bets are made of?"

"Not at all."

He chuckled. He couldn't help it. As the others chimed in, he remembered where he was and the other guests there. The thought sobered him instantly. "I guess I'd better get going," he said, suddenly feeling awkward and not knowing what else to do.

"But you've been invited to dinner!" Becca exclaimed, then glanced at Marissa. "You did invite him, didn't you?"

She nodded and Adam's heart was warmed by the look of regret that had made her eyes sheen when he'd offered to leave. "You did?" he asked.

"I did. You just didn't let me finish," she explained. "Besides, we have some unfinished business. Remember?"

"How right you are." How the hell was he going to propose with these people around? He had no choice but to remain and outstay them.

Dinner was more relaxed and enjoyable than he had imagined it could be. Marissa's guests were easy going and intelligent. He and Ted argued the new teacher testing that Texas was requiring; he and Becca discussed every little bistro that played jazz in Houston—and she knew all of them. And he watched Marissa as she went about hostessing. The food was delicious—some kind of chicken dish, vegetables in cheese and a giant tossed salad. The wine was a light Côtes du Rhône, a brand only someone who knew wine would have chosen. Even the Irish coffee served with light butter cookies was delicious. If he hadn't been anxious to talk Marissa into marriage—and his bed—he would have been reluctant to see the evening end.

But he wanted the hostess in his arms. Every time he glanced at her a frisson of excitement ran down his spine to rest heavily in the vicinity of his lap. Occasionally Ted glanced Marissa's way or cracked a joke and Adam was ready to fight. Perhaps that was the reason he went out of his way to talk to Becca; it kept him away from Ted's throat.

As Becca and Ted said their goodbyes, Adam kept his arm firmly around Marissa's shoulder. She was his and her fellow teachers might as well get that message right now. Perhaps they'd even broadcast the news: Marissa was taken. Hands off.

"You can take that smug smile off your face now," she muttered as she slipped from under his arm and stalked into the living room before turning to face him with the couch between them. "You succeeded in your efforts to make me look like some kept woman you dragged in off the street."

His eyes narrowed. Where was the sweet little woman who was laughing and chattering to her guests just minutes ago? "What are you talking about?"

"If I was a piece of beef on the hoof, you couldn't have branded me better," she said disgustedly, crossing her arms as if waiting for his apology.

"Good. I'm glad the point got across. I'd hate to think our teachers of today were so thickheaded they'd need someone to state the obvious."

She waited for him to say something else, but he continued to look at her blandly, waiting for her next move. "Is that all you have to say for yourself?" she finally asked, clearly at the end of her rope.

"Yes."

The silence stretched but he could see her wavering emotions. She didn't know whether to be mad at him or forget the whole thing. Slowly the bunched muscles in her slight shoulders sagged and her head drooped. She turned, staring out the wide expanse of window, hiding her face from his view.

But the pit of his stomach told him she was just seconds away from crying. With soft steps Adam came up behind her and circled her waist to pull her close to the front of his body, his warmth wrapping around her.

"I'm sorry," he murmured, resting his chin on the top of her head.

She leaned her head against his chest and gave a sigh. "No, you're not," she answered dejectedly. "You did it on purpose. You just didn't think it would embarrass me."

His arms tightened. "Don't tell me what I think," he growled, but it was a tender sound.

"Why not? You don't even know yourself very well, let alone me and my own set of morals or emotions. You thought that any woman would be proud to be *done for* as you've done for me. You can't seem to understand that instead of feeling secure because you want to take care of me and the baby, I feel cheap and used. You don't even know what goes on in my mind, even though you're constantly trying to second-guess instead of asking."

He turned her to face him, her expression hitting his gut like a mule kick. She was close to tears and the spunk that he had always admired was gone. He had stolen it away. He had meant to from the start but now, suddenly, he wanted to give it back to her. He wanted her the way she was before—willing to fight him on any level because she thought she was right and fair.

"You're right," he said slowly, as if it were a revelation to him. "So tell me. Explain to me. Help me to understand you, Marissa. You're a puzzle and no matter how I try, I can't seem to put you in the right order. Help me."

She shook her head and the curls grazed the top of his hands. "Just as you are who you are, so am I. No one can own me, rent me or buy me. I can give myself, but you can't take me. I'm not some business deal, Adam. I'm a person with thoughts and dreams of my own. And my dreams are just as important as yours."

She searched his face looking for understanding but found confusion instead. "If you were working on a business deal and another man got in your way, what would you do?"

"I'd remove him," he said promptly, wondering where she was going with that analogy.

"Exactly. Well, you're getting in the way of *my* business. Am I supposed to remove you from my life or sit back and allow you to run what is supposed to be my business?"

"I'm not getting out of your life, Marissa." His hands tightened on her shoulders.

"Is that fair?" she asked softly. "Why can't I be allowed to run my own business?"

"You don't have a business!"

"I do," she contradicted quietly. "My life is my business."

"The baby is my business."

She smiled sadly. "And that brings us to unfinished business. It sounds like a board meeting, doesn't it? Old business, new business, unfinished business."

"We're two people with more in common than business, Marissa, no matter what you think."

"No. You set up the business part of this relationship. I tried to make it a friendship, but obviously that won't work. Friends don't take advantage of friends, and you did a lot of that tonight."

"I was just trying to let—"

"—Let everyone know that I was private property," she finished for him. "But since I'm the property, it was my place to establish that. Not yours."

Slowly her words sank in. His legs turned to cement. "Marissa," he began, but she stopped him by stepping away.

"Just a minute." With quick steps she walked into her bedroom, appearing seconds later with a folder in her hand. She held it out to him. "Here's the contract you wanted me to sign. It's done. Now it's delivered," she said. "I think it's time that you left, too. Our unfinished business is completed."

"Just wait a damn minute." His voice was a growl that threatened to explode into a roar.

But she ignored the danger. "No, I'm exhausted and I need you to leave. If you have anything else to say to me, call me tomorrow afternoon. I'm sleeping in."

He didn't know what else to say. Without another word, he turned and left, leaving his heart in the hands of an exhausted woman who showed all the symptoms of hating him.

It wasn't until he reached his apartment that he remembered. This was supposed to be the night he proposed for the first time in his life. His hand clenched the already wrinkled folder, the cardboard biting into his palm.

So she had signed it after all. So much for integrity. Absently he opened the folder and checked her signature, only then noticing she had crossed out the "unlimited visitation rights" and had written in what was acceptable to her: "twice a week at an agreed-upon time, one weekend a month and one month a year—during the summer."

That little manipulator! He chuckled and his chuckle turned to laughter. He gave her ultimatums and she constantly turned them around. He'd state his opinions and she'd change them. And he was still standing in his apartment laughing!

So much for the best-laid plans of mice and men. He wasn't even sure which category he belonged in!

MARISSA'S FEET DRAGGED as she flipped out the lights and walked into her bedroom. Standing at the entrance, she stared at the bed as if seeing it for the first time.

She had never felt so alone before in her life. Tears glazed her eyes when she realized that as far as Adam was concerned, she was a piece of furniture, something to warrant protection, but not affection. "Damn!" she muttered to the empty silence.

She threw herself across the bed, cradling her head in her arms as she cried out her heartbreak. But a small part of her kept asking why she had expected more. She had known over three months ago, when she had made the fatal decision to go to bed with him, that it was all chance.

Just because she dreamed of a life with Adam didn't mean that he had to feel the same way. She knew it and had chosen to ignore it, allowing that little spark of hope to flame into a bonfire. Now she was paying for it.

6

"KNOWING YOU, MARISSA, you wouldn't have gone to bed with a man you didn't love." Marissa's mother was sitting cross-legged on the bed, her dark eyes delving into the myriad of expressions flashing across her daughter's face.

Except for her mother being taller, Marissa and she looked very much alike. Both were clad in jeans and bulky sweaters and both had long dark hair, only Jessica Pace wore hers in a low ponytail held by a large tortoiseshell clip.

Discussing the happenings that had led to Marissa's dilemma had kept them talking for over half an hour. She and her mother had retired to the bedroom while her stepfather stalked the length of the living room alone, pacing while his wife sorted out the emotional problems.

Although Marissa tried not to let her feelings for Adam show, they were impossible to hide completely. They shone from her eyes and were emphasized by her very posture. "Do you always have to be so understanding?" she teased in a husky voice.

Jessica leaned forward and clasped her daughter's hand. "I think we both know that my own knowledge is firsthand, honey. I've tried to impress it on you enough." Marissa stared at their entwined hands. "Perhaps too much."

Marissa's startled eyes found her mother's. "What do you mean?"

"I mean that there's a difference between love and lust, and from the look on your face, I'd say you found love. You passed through the lust stage and never blinked an eye. Now you're blaming this pregnancy on hormones because you're as frightened of love as I was at your age." She squeezed Marissa's hand. "But, honey, I was wrong. Don't let your happiness be consumed by fear."

"Are you sure you're not saying this because you're embarrassed by my pregnancy?" Marissa's voice was filled with both dread and hope.

Her mother shook her head. "I feel sad for you and regret the route that you've chosen. I chose it myself over twenty-four years ago and know a few of the problems ahead. But I could never be ashamed of you, Marissa. You're my daughter and I love you very much. The decisions you make must be yours because you have to lead the life those decisions dictate. Not me."

Marissa tried to smile, but couldn't quite pull it off. "I know. I'm just not sure I'm doing the right thing."

"You're sure he doesn't love you?"

Marissa nodded. "Oh, he's caring and concerned and kind, but he made it plain from the beginning that he didn't want marriage. He didn't want anything except access to his child." She bent her head, her long hair covering the sides of her face. "Besides, I know what marriage under these circumstances would be like. I don't want that, Mom. It was tough enough the first time around just to watch what you and Dad went through."

"And because Adam is caring instead of in love, he moved you in here, had you sign a contract to give you this condo, made a stipulation for child support and his visitation rights. All this to see a baby that hasn't been born yet," her mother stated dryly. "Honey, he could have gotten that from a court of law. He didn't have to do a thing except dump a settlement on you and he'd have all the rights in the world."

Marissa raised her hands to her head, shaky fingers rubbing her temples, hoping to erase the ache that seemed to be lodged there permanently. "I don't know anything anymore, Mother. I'm so confused. . . ."

Her mother gathered her into her arms and held her close, the way she used to when Marissa was a teenager. Her tears finally sprang out, the sniffles muffled by her mother's soft shoulder.

"Don't worry, honey," Jessica crooned. "It will all work out."

"And that's another thing," Marissa moaned. "I cry at the drop of a hat!" She pulled away, swiping at the wet streaks that stained her cheeks, trying to smile and reassure her mother.

Jessica chuckled. "That's perfectly normal. Blame it on imbalanced hormones. You'll do it for about another month and then you'll do it again after the baby is born." She stood and Marissa was again struck by the fact that her mother was a beautiful woman. And there was a hint of laughter that constantly lurked in her eyes, thanks to her husband, Gar. Marissa, too, loved Gar, as much or even more than her natural father.

"Now wash your face and come into the living room," her mother ordered softly. "I'm sure Gar is concerned enough right now. He wanted to tear Adam limb from limb earlier. Let's not give him any more cause for violence," she said with a smile.

"I'll be out in a moment," Marissa promised, stepping away from the bed and heading toward the bathroom. But once there she stared in the mirror at the girl who looked back.

What do you want? she asked herself, but she couldn't voice the answer aloud. Instead, it echoed in her head. *Adam's love.* But there was no way he could ever prove his love for her when he wanted his child, too. The two loves would always be intertwined and she'd never be sure if his feelings for her were real or an act he put on in order to gain access to his child.

She began to cry all over again.

It was half an hour before she pulled herself together and returned to the living room, and the laughter that echoed from there set her nerves on edge. What in the world was so funny? But the shock on her face when she entered must have stunned everyone else silent.

Her mother was seated on the couch, a cup of tea in her hands. Gar stood by the wide doors that opened to the patio, his salt-and-pepper hair glinting in the sunlight. And Adam was with him. They looked for all the world as if they were the best of friends.

Adam's smile slipped away as he strode toward her, reaching out to rest his hands on her shoulders. "What's the matter? Are you feeling ill?"

Her self-pity fled to be replaced by anger. "What are you doing here?" she demanded. "I don't remember inviting you!"

"The security desk told me your parents were here, and I didn't want you to face them alone," he said, his voice low enough for her to hear but not her parents.

"How considerate of you," she whispered back. "But you needn't have bothered. These are my parents, not the parole board."

He grinned. "You're always giving me hell for something, Marissa Madison. You might as well add this to my list of sins."

She ignored him, shrugging off his hands and walking toward the teapot on the coffee table. She tried to pretend her muscles weren't taut with tension. "I gather you've all met," she finally said to break the silent spell they all were under.

"And talked," Gar said, his eyes narrowing at her mother as if silently sending messages.

"And the verdict?"

"There is none." Gar held out his cup for a refill. "Except that we're worried about you and want whatever you want. As long as it's good for you."

She topped his cup. "Like brussels sprouts and carrots?"

"Like decisions based on fact, not fancy."

"What's that supposed to mean?"

"Nothing, dear," her mother interjected, giving her husband one of 'those' looks. "Stop being so suspicious."

Marissa couldn't help but glance toward Adam. How else was she supposed to act? Adam was here, and it seemed as if he had wheedled his way into her parents' good graces! She knew that thought wasn't fair, but she didn't care right now. Her smile was brittle. "So now that you've met the father, what do you think?" she pressed, knowing she was behaving like a child and unable to stop herself from doing so.

"Marissa . . ." Gar's voice held a warning in it.

Adam stepped closer to her and she felt as if the air she breathed were becoming scarce. "They think what I think—that you and I have a chance for a good marriage." Adam's words descended like a load of bricks hitting the room.

"What?" she asked stupidly, not seeing her mother's quick movement toward her, or her stepfather's dark look aimed at Adam.

"They believe we should get married. So do I." Adam's words were clear and concise.

Marissa's brain numbed. "I don't believe it," she finally whispered, her brown eyes wide with bewilderment. Her parents wouldn't do this to her. They wouldn't pressure her against her wishes! They couldn't!

"Marissa," her mother began.

"No!" she exclaimed, turning on her mother, her heart and heartbreak in her eyes. "You agree with him! I don't believe it!" She turned on both her parents. "After the horrible first marriages the two of you went through, you're now saying that you want me to make the same mistake?"

Her mother's dark eyes darted from Gar to Adam, then landed on her. "We want you to do what you want to do. But Adam says he loves you, and you've already admitted that you love him, too. Is it wrong to want your daughter to find happiness?" she asked softly.

Adam strode to her side, then stopped as if he weren't sure if he'd heard correctly. "You love me?" His voice was harsh with emotion.

Her chin tilted stubbornly. "Read my lips: We . . . are . . . not . . . get-ting . . . mar-ried."

"Why?"

Marissa's mouth opened, then closed and opened again.

Gar took her mother's arm. "I think this is our exit line. Show me the rest of the condo, Jessica," he said quietly, and then they were gone, leaving Marissa alone with Adam.

He touched her cheek with a finger, soothing her skin where the tears had run. "I love you."

"Really?" She gulped back the large lump in her throat, wanting to believe him, but knowing that her bubble would only be burst again. "Since when?"

"I don't know when. I just do." His finger traced a line to her mouth, parting her lips and grazing her teeth. His breath was warm, his gray eyes were even warmer. But her heart still sank to her toes. The look was lust, not love.

"No. You want to take me to bed. You want to pass some kind of test so that I'll change my opinion of your ability as a lover. You want a better rating than you think I gave you the first time. You even want a baby that you can call your own. But that doesn't mean you love me, Adam." Her voice was filled with regret.

"But I do," he said in a voice that was Southern soft.

"Then why the relief when you realized I wasn't asking for marriage? Why the contract? Why the separate apartments?" She shook her head before he could answer, knowing she couldn't handle his excuses. "No, you think it's the right and proper thing to do, especially since you've met my parents and realize we're all relatively nice. You know us personally now, and you're involved . . . for the moment."

His hand trailed to her throat, his thumb resting on the hollow where her pulse beat erratically. "And what makes you think I don't love you?" he asked, sounding almost detached and conversational.

"Because if you did you would have pushed for this earlier. You would have wanted me as your wife right away. No. This is a gut reaction to fatherhood. It will pass."

"And since when did you become Mrs. Freud?" he teased, still treating her as if she were a child.

She brushed his hand away. "Stop patronizing me," she snapped.

"I wouldn't dare." He chuckled, the hands that had caressed her face now resting on her hips. Then he turned somber. One hand crept forward and cradled her stomach. "But this baby is ours. I planted this seed when we made love. It took two of us and I want it to continue taking both of us to raise him."

"Her."

"Or her," he conceded. "I want you *and* I want the baby. Why is that wrong?"

"Can't you see?" She placed her hands on his chest in her earnestness. "I need to be loved, too. Maybe not by you, but by someone who thinks that I'm the only person in the world for him. The man I marry will tell me that by word, deed and expression. I *need* that."

He sighed heavily, pulling her toward him. "And I don't do that for you," he said, making the question a statement.

"No," she whispered into the hardness of his chest.

"If I did, would you believe me?"

"Yes. No. I don't know."

His arms tightened around her, letting her feel his physical need of her as much as his emotional need. "I'll prove it to you somehow, Marissa," he promised.

"You'll try, Adam," she said, looking up at him with all the sadness of centuries in her dark brown eyes. "But you won't succeed because the depth of love that I need for a marriage won't be there."

"We'll see," he murmured, his sculpted lips just inches away from the invitation of hers. "We'll see."

Then his mouth covered hers, slowly but firmly enveloping her in the sensuous scent, taste and texture of him. Her hands slid up his chest and she wrapped her arms around his neck as she strained to answer his unspoken questions.

You like my kisses.

Yes.
You love me.
Yes.
It's enough to begin with.
No. I need more. Much more.

He pulled away reluctantly, his breath short, his eyes dazed from the power of her kisses. "You've already admitted you love me. As far as I'm concerned, that's enough on which to base a marriage." She began to interrupt him, but he pressed his fingers against her swollen lips. "But I'm willing to do whatever it takes to convince you that I love you, too. So be prepared, Marissa Madison. There's a little magic I haven't worked out yet, but it's coming."

"Forget magic," she said. "You'd need a miracle to convince me your feelings are more than superficial. It's over, Adam." She walked out of his arms and across the room, fighting to regain her equilibrium. Good grief, she couldn't even think around him! "Please, try finding someone else to play with. When the newness of the chase is gone and this is over, I'm the one who'll still have to suffer the consequences. Not you—me."

"Damn," he swore softly under his breath. Her back was stiff with resolve and his fingers ached to follow the line of it. "You're the most stubborn woman I've ever met." He strode to the front door. "This is just the beginning, Marissa."

And with that promise or threat, she wasn't sure which, he was gone.

She plopped down on the bentwood rocker and stared at the place where he had stood. Her whole world was upside down and she didn't know what was what anymore. If the situation weren't so tragic, she'd laugh.

The man she'd loved for more than three years, the father of her child, had just proposed to her and she'd turned him down because of her own insecurities.

She was nuts!

The silence pounded in her head. She willed herself to relax, to end the buzzing in her ears. Finally she was able to hear the drone of her parents' voices in the other room, quietly talking. Wherever they were, Jessica and Gar found enjoyment in each other's company. Right now their closeness emphasized Marissa's own loneliness.

She rocked back and forth with jerky movements, praying for some kind of peace from her frantically scurrying emotions. When none came she stood, leaving the chair rocking by itself behind her.

"Mother?" she called, needing her parents to keep her from her own thoughts.

"Is it over?" Her mother popped her head around the bedroom door and grinned at her.

"Is what over?" she asked tiredly, wondering if she had fallen down Alice's rabbit hole.

"World War Three."

"No, but the hydrogen bomber just left."

Her mother walked into the room and gave her the reassuring hug she needed. "Honey, he loves you. There's nothing wrong with that."

"And how can you tell it isn't just words that were spouted to get what he wants?" she muttered into her mother's shoulder. She wouldn't cry. She wouldn't.

"How does anyone know? None of us are given written guarantees. But he's trying to reach out to you. Isn't that a form of love?"

"I used to love my cat, but it wasn't enough to base a marriage on," she snapped, then regretted her runaway tongue when she saw the hurt on Jessica's face. She sighed, touching her mother's hand in silent apology. "I don't know anymore, Mom. I just don't know."

Jessica leaned back and stared at her daughter. "You're too close to the problem," she announced. "Just remember this. He came into this apartment knowing we were here. That took a lot of courage. He also told Gar that he wanted you to marry him."

Marissa's laugh was as sharp as broken glass. "That was probably so Gar wouldn't kill him on the spot," Marissa tried to joke, wiping her tears away.

"Why would he do that? Gar was once in the same position as Adam is now. If anything, he understands what Adam is going through more than either of us does."

"But Adam didn't know that."

"I think Gar guessed even before Adam admitted his love."

"Oh, Mom! You're making me even more confused!" she moaned. "And you're a romantic who believes that everything should turn out with love triumphing over all."

"Take your time, 'Rissa," her mother said gently, ignoring her daughter's comment. "Just don't turn your back on something that could give you happiness. Don't be stubborn."

Marissa gave a watery chuckle. How many times had she been told that when she was growing up? Too often to count. "I'll try, Mom. I'll try."

"Can I come in, now?" her stepfather's handsome head appeared from behind the bedroom door.

"You might as well, Garner. It's got to be a strain on your ears to listen from that distance," Jessica teased, and Marissa wished they could both be held in a great big hug. Despite her problems, she was still the luckiest girl in the world to have the parents she did.

ADAM LEANED BACK in his desk chair and stared at the ink blotter in front of him. He had signed the papers his secretary put in front of him without checking the fine print, something he had never done before. Three months ago he had almost lost everything, and he'd had to work night and day for the past three months to save it all.

But now apathy concerning his business seemed to permeate his very being, and he knew the reason: all his thoughts were consumed with Marissa. The scene this morning played in front of his eyes. A fist had hit his gut when he had been told she loved him, but now he wondered why he was surprised. He had known all along that she wasn't the kind of woman to sleep with a man without having deep feelings for him. He had just chosen to ignore it because he hadn't wanted to admit the attachment he felt toward her.

But now everything was out in the open. He wanted Marissa as his wife and he was going to get her if it was the last thing he did! Whether she admitted her feelings or her mother did it for her, it didn't make any difference now. He knew of her love. There was no sense waiting for her to proclaim it—it was as good as said.

His thoughts were interrupted by the sound of determined steps heading toward his office. Without looking up he knew who it was—his father. Everyone had to put in his two cents worth, he guessed.

"What's this about you getting some filly pregnant?" his father righteously demanded from the doorway. The disapproving glare he gave his son was almost comical.

"If you're going to butt into my business, at least close the door," Adam said calmly.

His father stepped in and shut the door with a hard thud. "Is it true?"

Adam's eyes narrowed on the dapper man who had claimed fatherhood only after his son had grown into a success. "Yes."

"What's she demanding? Money? Marriage? Both?"

"What's it to you? It's my money, my single status that would be changed. Not yours." He couldn't keep the animosity out of his voice. Father or not, he didn't like the man and his uncaring attitude toward life in general and women in particular.

His father stood even straighter and Adam noticed his new suit. With his grayed hair and distinguished features, the gray suit and red tie complemented his assumed air of wealth. He was a ladies' man through and through. And Adam would probably find the clothing bill in next month's statement. "Don't do it, boy. She'll grab everything you've got and make you pay for it the rest of your life."

Adam grunted. "Don't worry, Dad. She doesn't want my sacrifice. She wants me out of her life. And the child's."

His father relaxed visibly. "Good. At least you don't have to worry about community property and giving her your blood for the sake of a brat."

"Was I a brat?" Adam's soft voice stopped his father's next words.

Surprised, his father took a moment to regain his composure. "Look, I know I wasn't too much of a father when you were small, but babies are for women to take care of and men to admit to. When you grew up, I did right by you."

"What a unique philosophy," Adam commented dryly, barely concealing his disappointment in the man he was supposed to call father. They had never been close. Only when Adam had made his money had his father even bothered to own up to the fact that he had a son. And with the acknowledgement came Adam's flow of cash. "Do you think all fathers adhere to that?"

The older man sat down on the leather chair across from his son, careful not to mar the pleats in his suit pants. "You turned out all right," he said, defending himself. "You've had more experience with life than most your age." He waved his hand in the air to indicate some of the more expensive paintings on the wall. "And you've done more than good for yourself. You've had the success that was denied me."

"Is that so?" Adam leaned back, his eyes widened as if he hadn't heard this speech a hundred times before. "Could that be the difference between working and wishing?"

His father sighed, hurt visible in his blue eyes. Adam didn't know if it was fake or real. He didn't care anymore. "You hurt, Son. I did my best for you. I stayed with your mother because I knew it was best for you."

"You took me to a whorehouse at the tender age of fifteen to ensure that I'd know about sex. You taught me how to drink, how to swear and how to appreciate the finer points of a feminine figure. I'll give you credit for those things. Nothing else." Adam threw down the pencil he'd been holding in his clenched hand. "You made home life miserable. Mother was miserable."

A picture of Garner and Jessica Pace flitted through his mind. Their love wasn't an act put on for the benefit of others. They loved each other, and they loved Marissa without trying to possess her. They were close and didn't mind showing it. Their relationship was something Adam envied....

His father's voice intruded on his reverie. "So was I, boy. Your mother wasn't the easiest woman in the world to get along with. She daydreamed her life away, praying she'd never have to face the coldness of reality. Do you think it was easy to live with that?"

Adam stood, unable to discuss his mother with the man on whom he blamed her death. "That's enough. I have an appointment, so we'll have to discuss this at another time."

His father stood, too, and they faced each other with the width of the desk and a thirty-two-year life span between them. "Just don't get caught, boy. I don't want you to be miserable the rest of your life because of one small mistake. It isn't fair."

One small mistake. From his point of view, small was relative. "Was I a mistake, Dad? Is that what happened to you and Mom?"

He shook his gray head. "No, Son. But by the time I realized my error in marrying your mother, she was pregnant and I had no choice. Not in those days. But today things are different and you don't have to marry to raise youngsters. Besides, you don't even know if it's yours."

"Where did you get your information?"

The older man dropped his eyes. "I have my sources."

"Mike's secretary," he guessed and saw the flush on his father's neck that confirmed it. "Isn't she a little young for you?"

"She's thirty-seven."

"And you're sixty-five."

"It's none of your business."

Adam ran a hand around his neck. "You're right. It isn't my business. And my relationship with Marissa isn't any of *your* business."

"But . . ."

"We'll discuss this some other time," Adam stated firmly. He reached for his suit jacket, ignoring the man who stood indecisively in the middle of his office. "See you later," he said, practically running out of the room and leaving behind that which he resented the most . . . the traits that had been passed on to him.

He slid into the heat of his car but didn't start the engine immediately. As usual, his first thought after a discussion with his father had been that the man had a horrible attitude concerning the raising of a child who was supposed to grow into a successful, well-rounded person. But it was the second thought that had stopped his movements.

Would he make a better parent for his own child? Would he care in all the right ways and lead his child into adulthood with as much guidance and as little possession as possible? He didn't have an answer, only a prayer.

For the first time he had to admit that as far as women were concerned, he had followed in his father's footsteps until knocked senseless by Marissa—a pocket-size Venus who set his mind on fire with thoughts of the home and love he'd always craved. A craving he'd never really acknowledged until now. . . .

Marissa didn't believe in miracles, but he was going to try like hell to deliver a little magic.

MARISSA'S PARENTS LEFT the following afternoon, and as soon as the door closed behind them, she began cleaning. It was what she always did when she didn't know what else to do. The activity kept her mind from buzzing with the problems confronting her.

Garner and her mother had been wonderful. They were worried and more than a little concerned, she knew, but they would never desert her because she had made a mistake. If she needed help, they were there with both love and money.

No. They weren't the problem. Adam was. Now that he knew she loved him, he'd stop at nothing to get his way. He wanted the baby for whatever reason and was willing to use emotional blackmail to get it.

She didn't know what to do.

The boom of the old vacuum ricocheted through the rooms as she pushed the machine back and forth over already cleaned carpets. When a stitch in her side forced her to stop, she dusted and polished and cleaned every piece of furniture, every windowpane.

And still there was no relief from the clamoring questions in her head.

She loved Adam and felt like a fool for being so scared of what he was offering. Was her mother right? Was it past experiences, not present circumstances she was running from?

Plopping on the couch, she stared at the now drooping ficus to the side of her. "You don't feel up to this, either, do you?" she asked the treelike plant. "I'll give you water and hope for the best, okay? It's all I can do at the moment." The air conditioning came on and the plant gave a shudder. "And that's all I can do for me, too," she admitted to the yellowing leaves.

On the way to the kitchen for water, she made her decision: she would not agree to Adam's proposal, even though she knew he'd ask again. Something deep down inside her told her that he might think he loved her now, but he would grow to feel trapped and hate her later.

That would be worse for her than never tasting his love at all.

He probably wouldn't appreciate her decision until later, when he came to his senses and realized that taking on a family wasn't just providing money. A family meant being there when someone got sick, when problems hit, when babies spit up.... And it meant giving constant emotional support to your spouse and child. She ought to know—that support was the one thing she never saw her own father give and the single, most badly needed item on her happiness list.

Adam wasn't prepared for that. He probably had grandiose but not too realistic dreams modeled on the traditional home life he'd obviously had, and she would be stifled in that atmosphere.

Marriage would be disastrous for all three of them.

With that decision made, she felt better. Not great, just better. She ignored the pocket of emptiness somewhere around her heart, for that feeling certainly was easier to take than the pain Adam could fill her with if things didn't work out. He wouldn't think so now, but she was doing him a favor.

As time passed he'd drift away from both of them altogether. Just as her own father had.

While Marissa was cleaning and pondering Adam's fate, he was paying a visit to an exclusive baby shop in the Galleria shopping area.

Looking around, he noted that everything seemed to be white with splashes of crayon colors. He didn't have the slightest idea where to start.

"May I help you?" A middle-aged woman greeted him kindly, seeming to guess his problem.

"Let's start with cribs and then you can show me what else I need for a baby."

"Boy or girl?"

"Boy," he stated promptly, then hesitated. "I think."

"Price range?"

"Whatever I like."

She smiled, and he could tell she was as excited about choosing the furniture as he was confused. "Let's start over here, shall we?" she asked, walking toward a long aisle of cribs that seemed to come in all shapes and sizes.

7

JULY QUICKLY SLIPPED into August, and August ran through the heated summer days just as fast until the cooler evenings of September arrived. Shortly after her parents' visit, Marissa found a part-time job in a small insurance office not far from home. She worked four afternoons a week. Typing and filing weren't her favorite things to do, but it beat staring at four walls and wondering what Adam was going to try next. Her small but growing stash of money helped ease her mind. She was able to pay her way, if only for a little while.

Ever since her parents' visit, Adam had gone out of his way to be sweet to her. Spring flowers were delivered regularly once a week and they were so beautiful she didn't have the heart to refuse them, even realizing it was the work of his secretary. Certainly Adam wouldn't take care of small items like choosing flowers.

He ordered dinner to be delivered at least twice a week—all her favorites and some dishes she had never tried before but quickly loved. Occasionally he would call and invite himself over. On those nights he'd begin with a chaste kiss or two, but never attempted more than that. It drove her to distraction waiting for him to pursue what those promising kisses could ordinarily have led to.

Then there were the evenings when he stayed away, and those meals were never as enjoyable—she spent the entire time wondering where he was and who he was with, only telling herself it didn't matter after having fallen into the pit of self-pity.

She missed him when he wasn't around, and she was afraid of him when he was. His overwhelming power over her happiness struck fear in her heart. She was becoming used to having him around, used to the fact that he thought about her as much as she thought about him, used to his kisses, his touch. But he hadn't said another word about marriage, and she was torn in two about that, too.

A thousand doubts assailed her when she was in one of her down moods. At this time in her life she was so vulnerable emotionally, she ran a gamut of insecurities she realized she'd never experienced before. Was she growing ugly as the baby grew? Was she losing the art of making scintillating conversation? Was he feeling the responsibility of parenthood, secretly glad she wasn't pressing for the marriage he had originally offered? She didn't know, and not knowing the answers was almost as frustrating as the man himself was.

The intercom buzzed from the desk downstairs and she walked over to it, pressing the button. "Yes, Arthur?"

"There's a rather large delivery here, Miss Madison. Three men are on their way up with it now."

"Delivery? I didn't order anything." A frown wrinkled her brow as she tried to think what it could be.

"Mr. Pierce ordered it, ma'am."

Dinner? Flowers? Balloons? There was no use guessing. She'd see it soon, whatever it was. "Thanks for the warning."

But when she opened the door, she didn't believe it. Three men stood there, each with a large dolly holding crates of...she didn't know what. "Are you sure you're supposed to deliver this here?"

The first man nodded, smiling as he glanced at the evidence of her condition. In the past two weeks she had bloomed to the point of wearing maternity clothes. "Yes, ma'am. This is from the Contented Baby furniture store."

Her eyes widened as she opened the door fully and directed them to the spare bedroom. The last man turned around. "This'll take about an hour to set up, ma'am. These cribs are getting harder and harder to assemble."

She nodded, then walked directly to the phone. Punching out Adam's number was a feat—her fingers were shaking so badly that she had to try three times before getting it right. But when his secretary informed her he was out, she shook even more. "Please have him call me as soon as he returns," she managed.

"Will do, Miss Madison. I'd have my head chopped off if I did any less." The older woman chuckled. "You're to have access at any time of the day or night."

"I'd like to have access to his neck so I could choke him," she muttered direly.

His secretary chuckled again. "You might have to stand in line."

When the men left, she walked into the baby's room for the first time. Slowly, she calmed down.

It was beautiful. The crib was a natural oak varnished to a high gloss to highlight the grain. The dresser and baby changer matched the bed. On the floor were bright-colored clowns holding balloons. They were made to march across the walls where the baby could see them. A large package of hooks lay next to them, ready for a hammer to hang the clowns wherever she wished.

The mattress and crib pad were already set up, the crib pad matching the clowns sitting on the floor. They were darling. . . .

She covered her now growing stomach with her hand. "Damn you, Adam Pierce," she said around the large lump of emotion stuck in her throat. "Damn you for being so nice!"

It was less than an hour later that Arthur called up again to let her know dinner was on its way to her apartment. This time it was fresh seafood from one of the well-known restaurants in the city. She should *never* have opened her mouth two days ago and told Adam how much she loved shrimp and broiled fish!

As the sun set, she waited expectantly for Adam, praying he'd return in time to have dinner. But after a half hour, disappointment set in. He wasn't going to join her.

She missed him, but was only willing to admit it to herself. Halfheartedly she peeled a fresh jumbo shrimp and wondered where he was and what he was doing. And who he was doing it with . . .

ADAM PUSHED for one more lap in the Olympic-size pool before giving in and hanging on to the side while he caught his breath. No one else was in the gym or pool area at this time of day—they were all sane enough to be in their apartments eating dinner.

Except for Adam.

He was swimming for dear life and praying that Marissa's fury had dissolved enough for him to visit her later. He'd even sent dinner up in the hope of bribing her into a good mood.

But he could still imagine how angry she would be with him for picking out their child's furniture alone. She most certainly would have wanted a hand in it, but he hadn't thought about that until the set he had selected was already ordered from the factory.

He hadn't considered Marissa's tastes and feelings when he'd bought the stuff, he had just wanted to contribute to the well-being of his baby. He wasn't in the habit of thinking of others when it came to business, and the decision he made in buying the baby furniture showed that he was obviously not doing too well in the area of personal relationships either.

He leaned his head back and closed his eyes, drifting in the water. Marissa. For the past month he had tiptoed around her as if she were glass and he were wearing size-thirteen combat boots. Very carefully. And occasionally his tiptoeing had paid off. His reward had come with her first glance of delight, her smile that widened when he said something clever or nice. He even noticed a difference in her temper; it wasn't flaring half as much as it had been when he first moved her into the building. He must be doing something right.

He only saw her about a third as much as he wanted to, and even then he was on his guard. Oh, she had signed that stupid contract, but even with her own revisions it was breakable as hell. And he didn't know what he would do if he lost contact with her. She had become so important.

Face it, Pierce, he thought. Marissa is your pivot point.

He ducked his head underwater to cool his heated face. Every time he thought of Marissa stealing away in the middle of the night, he got hot with fear. The thought had taken root when he'd met her parents. What if she left? Went home to her family instead of remaining under his care? Or disappeared entirely?

That idea scared the hell out of him. It was also the main reason he was staying out of her life as much as he was. He didn't want to push her into making a rash decision.

He swam lazily over to the ladder and climbed out. It was time to face his fear. Wooing Marissa couldn't be done from afar. He'd have to get into the game and take his licks if he was going to stand a chance of winning.

Baiting the trap by teasing her with kisses and closeness, and then not following through was proving far harder on him than it was on her. In fact, it was driving him crazy!

Known for his persistence in the business world, Adam decided it was time to try the same tactics in his personal life. And that he might as well start tonight...

THE BENTWOOD ROCKER CREAKED as Marissa stood up to answer the door. She hadn't realized until that moment that she had been sitting in the dark. Flipping a light switch on the way to the door was all she could manage, for whoever was knocking was in a hurry. The rapping definitely commanded attention.

Wide brown eyes met dreamy gray ones as she opened the door and stood looking at the man who had been consuming her thoughts.

"Hi," he said slowly, his voice a deep baritone flowing over her like heavy cream.

"Hi, yourself."

"Think you might care for a little company?" He raised a dark bottle. "I brought my own wine."

"I'd love company." She moved aside, suddenly realizing she was still in the long apricot-colored robe she had donned after showering. She pinched the lapels together. "Give me time to change and then I'll join you. There's fresh coffee in the pot."

His hand covered hers, his knuckles grazing her throat. "Don't change. I promise I won't throw you over my shoulder and march you to bed, so don't change."

She became lost in the depths of his eyes. Her body swayed toward his and she caught herself just in time. Swallowing hard, she answered, "Okay."

He smiled, the corners of his mouth tilting up endearingly. "Okay," he repeated, finally removing the heat of his hand from hers.

Without thinking, she turned and walked toward the kitchen for the glasses. She needed any excuse she could find to avoid being in close proximity to Adam. But when she turned to enter the living room again, he was right behind her, his gaze burning her with its intensity.

"How are you?"

"Fine."

"And the baby?"

"Fine."

"Good," he said, dismissing the subject of health as he uncorked the bottle and poured them each a glass. Then he looked at her, raising his glass. "To a new life."

She nodded, then sipped and the cool liquid helped to ease her suddenly parched throat.

They drifted into the living room, and as usual, Marissa curled into the corner of the couch while Adam sat next to her, his body curved to face her. She watched him from the corner of her eye, waiting for him to mention the baby furniture. A peaceful lethargy had taken over her limbs and she wasn't going to start an argument tonight. Not on her own.

"How's your job going?" he asked conversationally.

Her brows rose. It was the first time he had mentioned it since he had told her not to take it, and she had explained to him quite clearly what he could do with his high-handed orders. "Fine."

"Everything's fine, then," he said dryly, but a small grin tilted his mouth again and she responded by sending him a dazzling smile.

"I like it," she said simply. "It makes me feel like I'm pulling my own weight, even though you're providing almost everything." She tilted her head and looked at him. "I'm saving most of my pay right now. It seems that I have this good fairy sending me delicious fully-cooked dinners almost every other night, so I don't have to worry about overextending my food budget."

He reached out and touched a coffee-colored tendril of hair that rested on her shoulder. "I've only given you a place to live, Marissa. It'd be empty without you." He wanted to say that he'd be empty without her, but the words refused to come.

"And what about all the dinners? The flowers? The balloons?"

He glanced around. "Where are they?"

She chuckled. "The balloons last at least a week or two so I keep them in my bedroom. They're papering my ceiling." She motioned toward her small table in the kitchen. "And the last flower arrangement is on the table. You must not have noticed. The one by the rocker is from the week before."

"Do you like them?" His fingers grazed the slender side of her neck.

"I love them." *Because they came from you.*

"I loved sending them. I've been trying to pick out a slightly different bouquet every day. It's become a game."

"Your secretary didn't order them?"

He shook his head, smiling. And then the conversation lapsed into a comfortable silence.

Still playing with a strand of her hair, he waited for the subject of the furniture to be brought up. He didn't care if she was angry with him now; he was with her, touching her, and nothing could make him lose his temper.

Seconds stretched into long minutes as Marissa stared out at the patio and Adam stared at her hair. She knew he was doing it, but she didn't want to break the slender thread of contact they had.

"Marissa," he said, his voice a hoarse whisper. She turned her head slowly, finding his face just inches from hers.

His gray eyes burned her with intensity and fire and longing. Her own eyes mirrored his emotions. She longed to touch him, to feel the texture of his skin, breathe in the scent of him. Her breath caught in her throat.

Her lips parted in eager anticipation. Her eyes widened at his look. It was so tender, so comforting that she wanted to cry with the wonder of it.

"My 'Rissa," he whispered just fleeting seconds before he gently covered her mouth with his. His touch was like electricity hissing through her, and she moaned, not realizing immediately that it was she who had made the sound. His hand slipped around her neck, pulling her closer and seeking the shelter of her hair. The strong will that had always been such an integral part of her was melting like butter. There wasn't a coherent thought in her head as she moved toward him, seeking his closeness without realizing it.

She sizzled when he took her hands from her lap and placed them on his chest, rubbing them against the softness of his shirt. "Touch me, Marissa. Touch me like you did that night," he demanded in a whisper, and her fingers curled into the fabric.

When he placed his hand possessively on her hip and pulled her closer, she complied, mindless of the dangers involved. She felt as if she had been waiting for this to happen, and every day had been a disappointment. She loved him so much and yet could never touch or feel or look at him for as long as she wanted to. With shaking fingers she undid the top two buttons on his shirt, then slid her hand inside to feel the pounding of his heart and the warmth of his skin. The hair that spattered his chest, caused an erotic tingling in her palm that combined with those other sensations she had craved for what seemed like hundreds of years.

Another moan bubbled from her throat when he circled the tender flesh of her sensitive breast. A subtle thumb flicked over her budding nipple and she arched toward him.

Suddenly, his head snapped up. "What was that?"

She opened her eyes slowly, barely able to focus on him. "Hmm?"

"That thump." His hand left her breast to cover her belly and she blushed as she sought to brush him away, but he wouldn't let her.

"It's the baby," she explained, embarrassed. "She moved."

His eyes widened in stunned silence, then followed the downward path his hand had taken and stared at her belly. Marissa felt herself blush again. She should never have allowed this to go so far, never. . . .

"She moved," he repeated in wonder. "Will she do it again?"

"Probably." Just as she spoke, a tiny thud hit the palm of his hand again and his eyes became anchored to the spot. "My God." His voice was just a whisper.

"Did you think I'd swallowed a pumpkin seed?" Even though her tone was light, her voice was as husky as his. He was as awed as she was, and that knowledge made her love him even more. He cared.

"You're so small, the baby's so tiny. It seems impossible that there is a miniature person under my hand, Marissa, yet our child is kicking my hand."

She took a deep breath and felt the pressure of the baby just under her breast, then gave a soft giggle. "Oh, I have no problem remembering I'm pregnant, Adam. She reminds me all the time. My pants don't fit, my appetite requires odd things to eat, my body rebels in the morning."

His gaze was piercing. "Do you mind very much?" he asked, and she knew the answer meant a lot to him.

"No," she whispered, not finding the words to express whys and wherefores. "Not at all."

He closed his eyes as he took a deep breath. When he opened them again, there was a glistening sheen that magnified the gray. "How many miracles do you need before you accept me, darling? Isn't this a miracle just under my fingertips? Didn't a miracle of circumstances bring us together so I could plant the seed that grows so deep inside you? Wasn't it a miracle that it took root and grew, bringing us together again?"

"Adam . . ." she began, pulling away.

"No. You're not retreating this time, Marissa. This is real and it's happening now. I won't let you leave me here alone while you pull away to some other never-never land. We belong together, you and I." He took a deep breath, his eyes boring into hers and holding her in place. "I love you, Marissa. And I love our baby. Marry me."

Fear rushed through her at those words. She removed his hand from her body and stood up, her back to him as she stared into the fern-decorated fireplace.

"Marissa?"

"No, Adam. Please . . . don't." She was tired of battling him, yet knew he would never understand her reluctance. To him everything was clear-cut.

"Why? You love me. I know it."

"But you don't love me. I'd be miserable within a month and end up bitter. It wouldn't work," she added, turning toward him, palms up, imploring him to understand. "Don't you see, Adam? We'd probably be divorced in a year and I'd have to pick up the scattered pieces and try to begin again. You wouldn't have that problem. All you have to do is lose yourself in work and go on as you were before." She hung her head, staring at the carpet as she tried to put her deep-felt emotions into words. "But it wouldn't be that easy for me. I'd know I'd been a failure in the one thing I wanted most. I'd look at our child and remember you with her, remember us as a family. I don't think I'm masochistic enough to put myself through that hell."

"It doesn't have to happen that way, you know. It could work out and we'd both be happy," his voice was soft, cajoling.

She nodded. "Sure, we might. Until you met another woman and fell in love with her—really fell in love, instead of just feeling a sense of commitment because you made a mistake. As soon as that other woman comes along, you'd leave me quicker than you could spit. I couldn't handle it, I know it."

"Better not to have loved and lost than to have loved without security?" His voice was bitter, his frustration evident. "No one can guarantee forever, Marissa. They can only work toward it and hope that they make it."

"That's not enough," she answered, all the sadness of her choice in her voice.

He stood, his tall, broad form towering over her. "You want a life with no hurt, and there isn't any such life. No one can get away with not taking some chances and hoping things work out."

Her eyes brimmed with tears and she blinked to keep them at bay. She wanted to cradle Adam's head against her breast, she wanted to walk away and ignore the hurt that was coming when he really did fall in love with someone else. She wasn't for him; she knew it. He needed someone beautiful and sophisticated and able to fit into his type of high-powered, jet-set life—not a schoolteacher who would rather be a mother and stay home caring for a family. Marriage would prove her inadequacies too quickly. There would be no shielding herself against him.

"You're afraid of anyone getting close to you, aren't you?" he asked perceptively and she blanched at his words. "You're just plain afraid," he murmured almost to himself. "Who would have thought it. You're really a coward at heart."

"Please go," she said, her voice breaking around the lump in her throat.

Slowly, he shook his head. "No, my 'Rissa. I'm staying. If you can't give me your hand in marriage, I'll have to settle for your love."

"No." Her voice was a croak.

He nodded. "Oh, yes. I've tried everything I know to show you I love you. Everything but making love to you. Now I'm going to show you what I feel with my body. It's only fair, Marissa. You've decided to deny me the one thing I want: a commitment with a license. Instead, I'll settle for the verbal commitment you'll give me when you're lying by my side and whispering words of love."

"No."

"Yes." His eyes narrowed. "Just like you did the first time we made love and you thought I was asleep."

Her throat almost closed. "You heard?"

He nodded. "I heard, although I thought it was a dream at the time," he answered grimly. "And I'll hear it again, if it's the last thing I stroke from you."

"I won't let you," she protested, but her denial was hardly heard as he leaned down and touched her lips with his. He touched her nowhere else, but her whole body sang with desire. His mouth teased hers, barely brushing her skin, and she longed—deep down—to creep into his arms and lose herself there.

His lips settled on hers, moving slowly, sensuously. Teasing thoughts emerged of another time when he had stroked her into loving until she could hardly think.

Her chaotic emotions caused havoc. She craved his touch so badly. What was wrong with grabbing happiness when it was right in front of her? All the future pain in the world didn't matter when she could have Adam now—if only for a little while.... "Adam," she whispered as his magic swirled around her.

"Yes, Marissa. Oh, yes," he whispered in return, finally wrapping her in his arms and holding her close to the hardness of his body. She could feel his passion, his heat, his hardness and she reveled in it even as she had protested against it. "You're mine. You don't know yet, but you'll always be mine."

She didn't know if he was begging or insisting, but she wanted him. Oh, how she wanted him! She'd been so alone and lonely these past five months, feeling as if she were encased in a bubble world where no one could see her or touch her, but from which she could look out and see ... and feel ... and want....

He swung her into his arms, carried her to the bedroom and, laying her gently on the bed, quickly stripped off his clothes and threw them to the floor. Promising and threatening, his eyes held hers, and a tingle zipped from her head to her toes in heady anticipation.

Then he was beside her, holding her, crooning in her ear. His breath was warm against her skin. He held her swelling breast and she tried to shy away. No longer slim, she was suddenly filled with a shyness at him seeing her ungainly body.

His hands circled her head, tilting her to face him. "No, Marissa. Don't," he whispered, his voice rough with emotion. "You're a part of me. Mine. And the baby is, too."

"I'm big," she moaned, shoving at his shoulder.

"You're so tiny I could fit you in my pocket, with or without our child."

"I feel . . ."

"Awkward? Beautiful? Fat? Sensual? Like the most loved woman in the world? I vote for the last one, but love is in the eye of the beholder," he teased huskily and brought a light chuckle from her. Then he frowned. His hand fanned away a wisp of hair from her cheek. "I won't hurt you or the baby, will I?"

Her eyes softened. "No."

"There's so much I need to read up on, to learn. My education has apparently been sadly lacking in certain areas."

"I'll see what we can do about that." He was so concerned, so worried, and she smiled, suddenly relaxed. "But be warned, she might take a potshot at you," she cautioned. "Our child becomes restless easily."

"In that case," he whispered in her ear as his lips tickled her earlobe, "there are a few other tricks to this trade that come to mind. We'll try them all...." His lips came down to hush her thoughts, his tongue showing her what his body wanted to do.

He grazed the hollows of her collarbone, trailed down to find the full-bloomed nipple that was thirsting for his mouth. He captured it, drawing deep sighs from Marissa. "Someday, darling, I'll do this and taste your milk. Our baby's milk."

Nerves of pleasure came awake and stirred through her body as she conjured up the picture of his word image.

His fingers sought and splayed her legs, seeking her moistness and playing her like a soft-toned guitar. She arched at the gentle but incessant beat, rising to gain even greater contact with his hand, but he held back. "Easy, darling. Easy," he crooned, pleasure with her response in his voice. "Just let it come."

Her heart was in her throat, pounding to his rhythm. Not realizing anymore what she was doing, she held his head to her breast, her fingers tightening with every thrust of his hand.

"Is that good?" His tongue traveled to her other breast, intent on making her nipple quiver into a bud like the one in his hand.

"Mmm," she moaned.

"More?" he asked, his own breathing as harsh as hers.

She writhed beneath his touch. "More, please, Adam. More."

But when she thought she would crash and burn with the feelings he aroused, he stopped, slipping behind her.

"No, I—" she protested.

"Shh," he whispered in her ear before biting gently on the lobe. "It's all right. This way I won't poke our child in the eye. Trust me."

A chuckle burst from her mouth, but it ended in a moan as he slipped inside her, sheathing himself in her warmth. His hands cradled her femininity, continuing to create sensations that once more began to lift her toward the pinnacle.

"You are so sweet!" he muttered just before he plunged into her again. His body shuddered and she was caught up in his tremor, which seemed to sweep from his skin to hers almost instantly. "Now!" he rasped, and she mindlessly arched to his hand, feeling him fill her with his thrust as patterns of starbursts lit her mind. His moan combined with hers, and breathing in unison they slowly drifted back to earth from what seemed like the highest mountain peaks.

"So sweet, so good," he muttered, soothing the back of her neck with tender kisses while continuing to caress her breast and stomach. "So perfect . . ."

She drifted off to sleep in his arms with a sense of completeness she had never known before. Her last thought was that this was what loving Adam should be like.

Much later the bed shifted, awakening Marissa from her sleep. Forcing open one eye she watched Adam walk, beautifully naked, toward her bathroom. Still sleepy, she cuddled into the covers and tried to find slumber again.

But the lack of noise kept her awake. No commode flush, no shower noise, no running water. Just silence.

Her brow puckered, her ears alert for the slightest sound. Was he all right? Was something wrong? The first thought that popped into her head was that he hadn't liked making love to her, but she refused to allow it roots. He had held her afterward, cradling her in his arms as if she were a fragile piece of Wedgwood.

She reached for her robe, discarded by the side of the bed. Slipping her arms into the sleeves, she walked quietly but quickly to the bathroom. Testing the lock, she opened the door and peered through the darkness of the room.

No Adam.

She walked through the bath only to stop at the door to the baby's room.

Moonlight poured through the large double window to illuminate the room. Adam was bent over the crib, his arms braced on the rail to hold his head as he stared down at the colorful mattress and blanket there. Like a trail of stars, tears glistened on his sharply contoured cheeks.

Barefoot, she came up behind him. Twining her arms around his waist, she rested her head against his back as she sought to give him the warmth and comfort she instinctively felt he so terribly needed. She nuzzled her face against his skin, smelling the scent of him she loved so well.

He didn't move, but she could feel his muscles stiffen. "You should be in bed where it's warm," he said huskily.

"Tell me. Share it. Let me help," she murmured against his back.

He sighed and she could hear his lungs fill again with air. "It's nothing."

"Don't shut me out, Adam," she pleaded, her hands tightening against his stomach.

He sighed once more, turning to hold her in his arms as he leaned against the side of the crib. He held her securely, one hand wrapped around her waist, the other pulling her face to his chest. He rested his chin against the top of her head. "We're having a baby," he announced softly.

"Yes."

"It's a miracle. We've done something that thousands of other people have done, but this time it's special. It's our baby."

"Yes."

"And you'll be a terrific mother. I wonder—will I be as good a father? Wanting isn't always enough. It's one hell of a responsibility and the biggest challenge of my life."

"We'll make mistakes, Adam. Both of us, and lots of them."

His arms tightened. "But you *care*. You feel and seek and hurt for truth. You don't hide your head in the sand and pretend that what you see is all there is."

She raised her head, seeking and gently following the line of his jaw with her fingertips. "Who did that?"

He grunted, his eyes staring above her head as if seeing another scene. "A woman I know. A mother who lived in a superficial fantasy world. I used to look in the windows of other kids' houses and know that I'd never live in one like theirs because their lives were different, better than mine. When I grew older I realized I never really wanted a house because I was afraid I'd never find what others had."

He sighed, absently brushing her back as he tried to recapture and replace the past in its proper slot. "If our apartment was clean, then the people living there were clean. If dinner was perfect then the people who ate it obviously didn't have any problems. Everything had to look right, not necessarily be right."

"Poor woman."

His eyebrows arched as he looked down at her for the first time since she'd entered the room. "Why her? Why not pity those who lived with her?"

"Because she chose to pretend a perfect life rather than live. Houses or apartments, it really doesn't matter. What matters is the people who live there. I won't do that, Adam. I'll have messes on the floor from the baby playing. I'll have mud in the sandbox. When you come to visit, the house will look like a play zone, not like something from *House Beautiful*."

His knuckle grazed her cheek. "I'm glad," he said simply. "I couldn't have picked a better mother for my child." He pulled her back into his arms with a sigh, feathering her brow with a kiss. "Thank goodness."

Her heart sank; his words underlined why she couldn't marry him. He wanted her for all the right reasons except one: although he made love to her, he didn't love her—madly, passionately, forever.

Instead, she fit the bill as wife and mother.

This time it was her turn to shed tears.

8

"COME TO BED," she whispered, her arms tightening as she led him back through the bathroom to her own bed. She ignored the sensation of his lean, muscular body leaning against her. This wasn't the time. . . . "You need sleep."

"Umm," he said, slipping between the covers, then turning to fold her into his arms and hold her close to his body. "I love this bed. I'm changing my king-size one for a single."

"Why?" she yawned as she rested her head against his lightly furred chest and curled her arm around his midriff.

"Because this is smaller. You're forced to stay close to me." His voice was sleepy, his tone deep with satisfaction. "There's so much to do tomorrow," he murmured before sighing deeply and falling into slumber.

But Marissa's eyes wouldn't shut. She lay quietly in his grasp as her thoughts kept churning. The woman he spoke of was obviously his own mother which explained so much about his attitude toward women. He had received all the necessary care for his body, but no one had bothered to nourish his emotions. Unless his father . . . She'd heard that his mother had died and his father depended upon him for money. Other than that, she knew little.

Still in sleep, he moved his hand to curve around her back, and she held her breath, wishing him awake as powerfully as she wanted him to continue to sleep.

The truth was she didn't know what she wanted anymore. Adam had upset her equilibrium so much that she was afraid to make a decision in case she was acting on emotion instead of logic. In her befuddled state of mind, any decision could be a wrong one.

The only two things she really knew was that she loved Adam and she wanted this baby.

Slowly, her eyes drooped closed and she slept, contentedly snuggled against the radiating warmth of Adam.

When she awoke she was alone. Sun blazed into the room, shining on her face and telling her that it had to be almost noon. She moaned, rolling over to escape the sun's rays, but it didn't work. The whole bed was bathed in sunshine.

The sound of muffled words filtered through the closed bedroom door and she cocked her head toward it. It did no good, the sound was still there, but the words were garbled. After wrapping her robe around her and tying the sash just below her breasts, she sat back down on the side of the bed.

Obviously Adam was in the living room talking on the telephone. If she walked out there and confronted him, what would she say? She didn't have the faintest idea.

The more
you love romance . . .
the more
you'll love this offer

FREE!

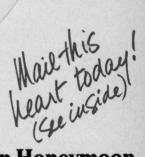

Mail this heart today! (See inside)

**Join us on a Harlequin Honeymoon
and we'll give you
4 free books
A free makeup mirror and brush kit
And a free mystery gift**

IT'S A
HARLEQUIN HONEYMOON—
A SWEETHEART
OF A FREE OFFER!
HERE'S WHAT YOU GET:

1. **Four New Harlequin Temptation® Novels—FREE!**

   Take a Harlequin Honeymoon with your four exciting romances—yours FREE from Harlequin Reader Service. Each of these hot-off-the-press novels brings you the passion and tenderness of today's greatest love stories...your free passports to bright new worlds of love and foreign adventure.

2. **A Lighted Makeup Mirror and Brush Kit—FREE!**

   This lighted makeup mirror and brush kit allows plenty of light for those quick touch-ups. It operates on two easy-to-replace batteries and bulbs (batteries not included). It holds everything you need for a perfect finished look yet is small enough to slip into your purse or pocket—4-⅛" x 3" closed.

3. **An Exciting Mystery Bonus—FREE!**

   You'll be thrilled with this surprise gift. It will be the source of many compliments, as well as a useful and attractive addition to your home.

4. **Money-Saving Home Delivery!**

   Join Harlequin Reader Service and enjoy the convenience of previewing four new books every month delivered right to your home. Each book is yours for only $2.24—26¢ less per book than what you pay in stores. And there is no extra charge for postage and handling. Great savings plus total convenience add up to a sweetheart of a deal for you!

5. **Free Newsletter**

   It's *heart to heart*, the indispensable insider's look at our most popular writers, upcoming books, even recipes from your favorite authors.

6. **More Surprise Gifts**

   Because our home subscribers are our most valued readers, we'll be sending you additional free gifts from time to time—as a token of our appreciation.

   START YOUR HARLEQUIN HONEYMOON TODAY—JUST COMPLETE, DETACH AND MAIL YOUR FREE-OFFER CARD

Get your fabulous gifts
ABSOLUTELY FREE!

MAIL THIS CARD TODAY.

GIVE YOUR HEART TO HARLEQUIN

YES! Please send me my four Harlequin Temptation novels FREE, along with my free lighted makeup mirror and brush kit and free mystery gift as explained on the opposite page.

NAME _____
(PLEASE PRINT)

ADDRESS _____ APT. _____

CITY _____ STATE _____

ZIP CODE _____

142 CIH MDPG

HARLEQUIN READER SERVICE "NO RISK" GUARANTEE

— There's no obligation to buy—and the free books and gifts remain yours to keep.
— You pay the lowest price possible and receive books before they appear in stores.
— You may end your subscription anytime—just write and let us know.

PRINTED IN U.S.A

START YOUR
HARLEQUIN HONEYMOON TODAY.
JUST COMPLETE, DETACH AND MAIL YOUR
FREE OFFER CARD.

If offer card below is missing, write to: Harlequin Reader Service, 901 Fuhrmann Blvd.
P.O. Box 1394, Buffalo, NY, 14240-1394

BUSINESS REPLY CARD

First Class   Permit No. 717   Buffalo, NY

Postage will be paid by addressee

Harlequin Reader Service ®
901 Fuhrmann Blvd.
P.O. Box 1394
Buffalo, NY 14240-9963

NO POSTAGE
NECESSARY
IF MAILED
IN THE
UNITED STATES

Her face blazed at the thought of their lovemaking the night before. Five months pregnant and she had acted like a young monkey swinging playfully from a vine. Lord, what must he think! And he had been so tender, so loving, so wonderful....

"You're awake." Her eyes darted up to find Adam standing at the door, a steaming mug in his hands, a twinkle in his eyes and a teasing smile on his well-formed lips. "I thought I'd better check on you. You've been asleep for hours and hours."

She eyed him warily. "I didn't mean to oversleep."

"I kept you up half the night, you have to make up the difference somewhere." He walked toward her and she stiffened. He looked for all the world like a tiger stalking his prey. "Your tea, Marissa," he said, allowing the grin to transform his face.

She dropped her eyes to the cup, reaching out with both hands. It helped to focus on anything except the very real, very seductive Adam in front of her.

"How's your stomach?" His voice was honey soft and silk smooth.

It took a moment for the words to sink in. Her brows rose. "Fine," she said, surprised that she meant it. No rumbling, no jumping up and down until crackers were ingested. "Maybe the morning job will be a thing of the past."

"Maybe. Just take it easy when you begin walking . . . I don't want you getting upset."

The silence stretched as she sipped on her tea. She didn't know what else to say, what to mention or how to broach a subject. Suddenly she felt fifteen years old again and awkward.

"Marissa, we have to talk."

Here it comes. She sipped at the hot brew again, hardly noticing the scalding it gave her tongue. "What about?"

"About us."

"What about us?" He stood slightly to the side of her; if she raised her eyes she would be staring at the zipper of his well-worn jeans. A leaden heat coursed through her body at the thought.

"Look at me." It was a command, and she followed his orders, staring into night-gray eyes that seemed to lick her into sexual tension. "About our wedding . . ."

She placed the cup on her thigh, still holding it with two hands. "No."

His expression hardened to granite. "Yes. We're getting married and there'll be no arguments from you. Do you understand? Last night, when you came into my arms willingly, you committed yourself to me. From now on we're a pair."

"It's not fair," she whispered. "Don't do this, Adam. Please." She grabbed for the cup and stood, walking away from him. "You say I committed myself but you didn't mention doing the same."

He walked to her, reaching for her shoulders as if to force her to hear him without bolting away. "We'll get married and we'll be a normal, everyday family. I'll never give you reason to leave me, Marissa. I'll be just as committed to you as you are to me. I promise you."

She raised her chin and tried to quell the panic that was steadily building in her breast. "No more women? No more nights with the men? No more gambling or drinking or traveling all over the country at the drop of a hat?"

A muscle twitched at the side of his mouth. He crossed his heart and held up his palm as if taking a pledge. "No other women, no nights with the men. No gambling, and I'll drink at home with my wife. As for traveling, I can't guarantee I'll be able to stay at home all the time, but I'll try to rearrange my schedule so that I won't have to do it so often."

She bit her bottom lip to keep it from quivering. "I don't think I can believe you, Adam." Damn these teary moods she worked herself into!

His voice was firm. "I've never lied to you, Marissa. Besides, you don't have a choice. I'm setting the rules and you're going to follow them," he ordered.

Panic welled in her breast again. She had to do something, anything, to deter him from making the biggest mistake of their lives. A second mistake didn't correct the first one. She should know; she'd watched her own parents.... She fluttered her lashes and reached out to hold on to his arms, as if feeling faint. "Please... Adam."

In the blink of an eye she was in his arms as he strode back to the bed, slipping her down safely but reluctantly. "You're doing too much," he said harshly. "And you haven't eaten today. I told you I'd take care of you, but you make everything leave my mind. Stay here and I'll get some food together."

"No, wait," she said weakly, her hand drifting to his chest where the blue chambray shirt was unbuttoned. She loved the texture of his skin, the softness of his hair on her palm. . . .

"What is it, honey? Should I call the doctor?" His brow furrowed in concern as he placed a rough-palmed hand on her forehead, feeling for a temperature.

But the fever was inside, not out. And the antidote was him. She knew it, she just couldn't say it. "I'm fine, just a little dizzy," she managed, and she wasn't lying. Around him she was always dizzy. It was an automatic reaction to his presence.

"Stay here," he ordered, leaving the room. The tension he always built in her when he was around evaporated the moment he left the room. Seconds later she could hear the rattle of pots and pans from the kitchen. She wasn't hungry, but it didn't matter. She now had some time to think about what she was going to do. Her lashes drifted down and she fell into a light sleep.

Something or someone made her wake up and, startled, she sat up. Adam was at the foot of the bed, his eyes withdrawn and remote. "Awake? I just made soup and a sandwich. Maybe you'd better eat it now, before it gets cold."

She shook her head. Was this the same man who had proposed to her just minutes ago? It was hard to tell. Now his expression was as if etched in marble, his whole attitude withdrawn. She ran her hands through her hair, flipping the mass over her shoulders. "Thank you." She sounded overly polite, but she couldn't help it.

He pushed a tray toward her. "Eat up. I'll be back later."

He was gone before she could raise the spoon to her lips. Her shoulders sagged under the weight of the emptiness she felt. He'd been with her for almost twenty-four hours and she was already addicted to his presence. It wasn't fair. Listlessly she played with the food on her plate, eating only what was necessary to avoid a confrontation about her appetite; then she shoved the tray away and walked to the bathroom.

The warm shower felt so good it almost revived her sense of humor over the ridiculous situation she found herself in. He'd proposed and she was trying to say no, then he'd retired into himself and now she didn't have to bother making up ways to say yes. She wanted to talk to him, laugh, enjoy his company—forever. Until recently she hadn't known he had such a wonderfully wicked sense of humor, and she wanted to delve further into other unknown facets of his personality.

She slipped into a new pair of tan maternity slacks and then chose an emerald-green blouse she had always loved. Looking in the mirror objectively made her realize she wasn't as big and bulky as she sometimes felt. The blouse wasn't maternity and she still looked good in it. She piled her hair on top of her head, letting a few strands straggle in curled tendrils to her shoulders. A little makeup and she was ready to face the tiger....

Adam sat in the bentwood rocker staring into the fern-filled fireplace. When he heard her footsteps, he looked up, his expression somber and somehow very sad. Her heart fell to her stomach. Was he regretting his solution? Was he going to walk out of her life now that he had gotten what he wanted? The thought hurt so much, a pain seared through her.

"Sit down, Marissa."

She perched on the edge of the couch, placing her hands together in her lap as if in prayer.

"Last night..." He hesitated and the pain came again.

"I know," she said woodenly. "I understand."

His brows rose. "You understand what?"

She gave a small, choked laugh. "My figure doesn't exactly inspire lurid lust, even if you really did care for me. You don't have to apologize for having second thoughts the morning after."

His expression turned into a dark thundercloud. "What the hell do I have to do to make you believe I love you?" he gritted through clenched teeth, his frustration obvious. "I've said it, I've tried to show you in a thousand ways." He leaned forward, his body tense. "What will it take to make you believe it?" She couldn't answer. Her mind wouldn't work. He came even closer. "Tell me, Marissa. Give me some advice as to how to get through to such a thickheaded woman."

She stared down at her hands, unwilling to incur more of his wrath. But her own honesty wouldn't allow her to hide from the answer. "Tell the truth, Adam. Would you love me if I *weren't* pregnant with your child? A child you believe to be your son and heir?"

"Yes." His answer was clipped, definite.

She looked up, all her vulnerability and insecurity showing in her eyes. "Then why didn't you seek me out after our weekend together? Where *were* you for the three months after that? You never even phoned."

Her tone of voice, that little-girl-lost quality, wrapped him in sorrow. That one act—or lack of action—was the reason for their problems now. He'd known that all along, but for the life of him he couldn't think of a way to explain his badly dented ego without sounding like a kid whose candy had been dropped in the dirt.

He leaned forward and reached for her hands, pulling her toward him until she sat in his lap. The chair rocked slowly back and forth. A feeling of protectiveness surged through him. It always seemed to arise when she was around, getting stronger every day, just as his love did.

Her head rested on his shoulder and she stared at their entwined hands as she waited for his answer. The saddest thing was that whatever he said, no matter how cold or cruel his words were, it wouldn't matter. She'd still love him.

He sighed heavily. "Less than a week before our short affair, I'd lost almost everything I'd worked so hard for because I'd taken a chance and invested everything I could get my hands on in a bad oil deal. I didn't know if I was going to file bankruptcy or try again. I was so depressed and confused I couldn't think straight."

He gave the rocker a small push, his hands holding her as close as he could. She was comforting: sweet, sweet comfort. "Then you came along and made me feel like I was somebody again. You cared—not for my money, but for me. But after our night together, I got scared. Pure and simple scared by a five-foot woman with an independent spirit and a heart as soft as a cloud." He paused, his fingers moving restlessly in hers. "I'd just ended a relationship that had been going on for three years, and although it was nice in the beginning, it had become habit all too quickly. Then the habit turned sour. That's when you walked into my hotel room."

"I knew about Elizabeth," Marissa whispered. "She wanted children and you didn't."

"Wrong," he stated quietly. "She wanted a baby and I didn't want her to be the mother of my child."

"You didn't want me to be that, either."

"I didn't know much about you then, but I think I've always been looking for a woman I could trust and love and spend my life with. I just didn't consciously know it at the time. I wanted a woman who cared—for me and about me—and not about the size of the dollar signs in my checkbook. I didn't really think I'd find that kind of woman, Marissa. Then you came into my life and I panicked. I had woken up that morning and hadn't felt so good in a long time. You'd placed a hot towel on my forehead earlier and had set aspirin and a glass of water on my bedside table, then crawled in beside me and curled up next to me like a warm kitten. All without asking—without expecting anything in return."

"That's common courtesy, Adam. There's nothing different about that."

"That's where you're wrong again. But then I began to think about it. What if you did ask for something?

All my illusions would be popped like bubbles. And there was nothing I had to give at the time. I was too confused to know how to deal with it, too immersed in my own problems trying to rebuild my business. So I ran."

"Until I called you to meet me. Did you think the payoff had been demanded then?" She glanced at him, then stared at their hands again. He had such beautiful hands—long fingers with a sprinkling of hair trailing down from his wrists.

"Yes. But by then I didn't care. Three months of hard work had delivered results—big results—and I had my business back. Besides, I'd been thinking of you for so long that I *wanted* to see you again. I needed to know if you were as terrific as I thought you were." He held her tighter for a moment. "And then you told me about the baby."

"You were so cold."

"I was stunned." He chuckled ruefully. "It hadn't entered my mind that you'd come to me because you were carrying my child. We were so good together, so *matched*, that I dreamed of coming to you again as soon as I straightened out my life. When you called, I thought you'd decided you couldn't live without my fantastic prowess in bed. Instead, you told me I was Flash Gordon and you could have done without that experience."

"That's not what I said," she corrected.

He chuckled again, a husky sound that flowed through her like golden-warm brandy. "That's what I heard."

"I was hurt. You were so cold, so remote, and I was already scared to death of your reaction. I had gone over telling you in my mind again and again. I was afraid you'd throw a couple of hundred down on the table and tell me to get an abortion."

He lifted her face up to his, brushing her lips with a soft, butterfly kiss. "What would you have done?" he asked curiously.

"I would have gone to my parents for help. I knew they would stand by me, but I wanted us to be involved with our child. Together." Her eyes got that faraway look where sorrow dwells. "I'd been raised by one parent who cared and one who grew to hate us. I wanted more for my baby. I wanted you to *want* this baby as much as I did so we could raise her together, help her grow, love her. Even if we didn't love each other, I thought we could put aside our differences enough to work together."

"Instead, you got a man who hounded you to be a part of his life. And you were the one balking."

She twisted to face him fully. "Adam. If you still mean it, I want to accept your proposal, under one condition."

His gray eyes grew wary. "The condition?"

"That we have a long engagement. That we prove to each other that this marriage will work out."

"How long an engagement are you talking about? Honey," he said, his hand cupping her stomach tenderly, "you're already five months pregnant. Don't you think it'd be nice to be married when our baby is born?"

His voice held a note of laughter, but she couldn't smile in return.

"I think it's better not to marry at all if the marriage won't stand a chance of working. I don't want to be divorced a year or two from now. I want us to be forever."

"You don't care that the baby won't have a name?"

"The baby will have a name. Mine."

He sighed again. She was so beautiful, spirited, loving—and hardheaded. What choice did she leave him? He knew he'd accept the condition, but he had to have a little power play of his own, he deserved it. "On one condition."

Her eyes widened and he had the urge to kiss them closed and then trail kisses down to other parts of her body—that small mole that nestled just below her breast, for instance.... "What condition?" she asked huskily, and he thought for a moment that she could read his mind.

"That you don't keep me at arm's length. We spend time together, day and night, and really get to know each other. That the engagement is announced and be as binding as our marriage will be."

"Then it couldn't be broken."

"And that we'll either marry on or before Christmas. You should know then whether or not we'll work together."

She tilted her head to one side and her hair slid over her shoulder to curl beguilingly over her robe-covered breast. "Why?"

"Because I want to be married for Christmas. I want happy memories to build the rest of our life on, or at least no false hopes hanging around."

"Christmas," she said slowly, then nodded in agreement. "Okay. Deal." She stuck out her hand.

"Deal," he repeated, ignoring her offer of sealing the agreement. Instead he lowered his head, brushing her lips with his until he couldn't stand the teasing and molded her mouth to a perfect fit. Their breaths mingled, their tongues caressed and his heartbeat quickened.

He held her closer, wanting to absorb her into his very soul and never let her go. Her scent swirled around him, enclosing him in a sensuous curtain of desire. Passion flared up and burned brightly in the pit of his stomach. He knew she could feel him hardening against her, but as her breasts touched his chest, he realized that she was just as excited as he was. Her nipples burned his skin, warmed his insides like brandy. He pulled away, touching her forehead with his.

"Do you always seal a deal like that?" she asked breathlessly.

"No, this is a first," he admitted hoarsely. "Do you think we could complete this contract? A small smile tugged at the delicious corners of her mouth and he had to kiss them, too.

"I think it's the only way to handle this business deal," she answered softly as she stood and reached for his hand. "I'll show you the best spot to negotiate this agreement."

She led him across the living-room and bedroom floors, only to stop uncertainly at the edge of the bed. He stared down at her, cupping her heart-shaped face between his hands. "What is it, honey?"

A blush tinted her cheeks as she glanced down at her rounded figure. "I wanted to seduce you, but I'm afraid I'm not in shape for it," she finally confessed.

The laugh started in Adam's throat, echoing to a rumble in his chest. He pulled her into his arms, rocking her back and forth as he continued to chuckle. "So far you've done a damn fine job of leading me along, Marissa. You should know by now that I'd follow you anywhere," he said finally as he continued to hold her close to him. Possession was nine-tenths of the law, and he wouldn't allow anyone to take away what he so needed in his life. Marissa. His Marissa.

His eyes felt hot with love and tears, and an almost overwhelming possessiveness enveloped him. She couldn't leave him. Not now. Not when he stood a chance of having the only happiness he had ever known. God couldn't be so cruel. . . .

THEY SPENT the next two days together locked in Marissa's apartment. The outside world was just that— outside the patio where they could view it from afar, but not become involved with its day-to-day maneuvers.

Adam made one phone call to his secretary, telling her that he was out of town to everyone. She returned the call the next day to bring him up-to-date on who wanted what, and that was it. Marissa lived in her robe.

She cooked him all her favorite dishes. They watched two of her favorite old movies. He taught her how to play Nada, a dice game he had played as a child and had forgotten until now. He watched a football game while she baked a cake, filling the rooms with that magical scent of homey spices.

And they talked: politics, religion, personal beliefs. Nothing was sacred, nor were there too many times that one changed the other's mind. They agreed to disagree. Or to kiss and make up. Or to not pay any attention to the other's odd ideas. It all ended up the same way, in each other's arms with love and laughter shining from their eyes.

By the time Adam had to face the business world again, he felt as if he'd been on vacation for months—and yet not gone long enough.

He reluctantly retreated to his own apartment and was amazed to find it the same as when he'd left it. The furniture was the same, the newspaper neatly folded next to his chair. It was too clean, too pristine, too empty to be called a home.

Dressing quickly, he left for the office, forcing himself to take the elevator all the way down to the garage instead of visiting Marissa once more. A smile lit his eyes as he remembered leaving her this morning. She was still in bed, sitting up with her arms wrapped around her knees and her hair a glorious riot of curls that danced on her shoulders and back like mahogany ropes. Her eyes had been wide open and her lips tilted in a smile that wrapped his heart in happiness.

"I was thinking about Thanksgiving dinner," she'd said. "Thanksgiving requires bread dressing."

"Cornbread," he had teased, knowing what she was going to say.

"Bread," she corrected. "And cornbread. I'll make both."

He had leaned over, unable to stop himself, and kissed the tip of her nose. "I'll eat both."

Her laughter had touched the air like motes dancing in sunlight, and the sound still echoed in his ears.

He made it to the office in half the time since he had left later than usual and had missed the first rush of traffic. He filed that small fact away. That meant that he should always leave late. It would give him more time with Marissa. . . .

It was becoming a habit for him to sign papers without looking at them, he thought, but then reasoned that his secretary had always been efficient before. "Judi," he said as he handed her the last one. "I think it's time you had a raise."

"I'll take it," she said quickly as she reached for the stack of correspondence. "How much?"

"Are you underpaid now?"

"No, but I won't turn down a dime."

He grinned. "Is that what you're asking? A dime?"

"Not on a bet."

"Good, then we'll make it ten percent."

"Starting when?"

"Now."

Judi leaned her generous hip against the large mahogany desk. "Make if fifteen and I promise I'll keep all your calls at bay and never breathe a word of your whereabouts."

He couldn't help laughing. "Ten percent and you'll do the same damned thing."

She shrugged, grinning with him. "Okay, but it won't be as much fun."

"And call I.W. Marx and let them know I'm looking for an engagement ring. I'll be over there this afternoon."

"Right," she said, ambling across the carpet and walking out the door. Just before she shut it, she peered around at him. "By the way, your father's been here twice and says he's been to your apartment once. My bet is he'll find you sooner or later," she announced before quietly shutting the door.

"Let it be later. Much later," he muttered to himself as he went through the rest of the calls that he had ignored so far. He had enough pressing business to weigh him down without worrying about his father's bad debts.

He phoned Marissa and it took half an hour to set up a time for her to meet him at his office. First, he'd had to convince her that she needed an engagement ring or he'd call the whole trial period off. She didn't know it was a bluff—probably the biggest one of his life.

Work went at a feverish pace for the rest of the morning and through lunch. He was almost through when Marissa walked in the door, her dark hair shining, her face glowing and her walk . . . well, her walk should have been outlawed, pregnant or not.

"Am I early?"

"No, right on time," he said, coming from around his desk to sit on the edge and pull her to stand between his splayed legs. He needed to touch her, make sure she was really here. The morning had been filled with a thousand thoughts of her, interfering with everything he was supposed to be doing. He nuzzled her slender neck, his lips grazing the side of her ear, and he caught a whiff of her perfume. "Umm, you smell good."

"It's called bathing." She chuckled, but her hands still circled his neck to keep him close.

"It's called Marissa," he corrected, trailing kisses along the line of her jaw until he reached the sweetness of her lips. "And I'm addicted to it."

It was like kissing her after not seeing her for a year. Once more, he was amazed at how quickly he *had* become addicted to her.

She pulled back, her lips blushed and swollen from his own. "Don't you think we'd better go?" she asked huskily.

"What are you afraid of?"

She nipped at his jawline with her lips. "Your secretary walking in here and finding me on the floor with my skirt over my head," she teased.

There was something in her eyes that told him she was frightened. It couldn't be of him—he refused to believe that. But he'd seen that look enough in the past several weeks to know that whatever it was, she wasn't ready to tell him. He'd already tried that. All he could do was wait patiently and hope that she'd trust him enough to open that last door and let herself be vulnerable to him.

"You're right. We have a very important appointment and I'm not letting you off the hook just because you decide to flaunt your feminine wiles at me," he said, reluctantly pulling his arms away from the warmth of her. "You'll just have to wait until we get home for me to give you what you're asking."

He stood, and with her hand securely tucked in his, he strode to the door. It was time to do something, anything, but stay in the privacy of his office with a siren who had his heart so thoroughly trussed up.

9

THE ENGAGEMENT RING Adam chose fit her finger as if it had been made for her. She couldn't help glancing down at it at least a hundred times during the ride between the jeweler's and a small Parisian restaurant nearer home.

His hand covered hers, fingers outlining the shape of the ring. It was a marquise-cut diamond, and as far as she was concerned, cost far too much, but he had overruled her objections. And she loved it.

"Happy?"

She smiled brilliantly, amazed at the way his eyes narrowed and warmed when he looked at her, sending messages that made her own blood run heated and quick. "Yes."

He pulled into the parking lot of the restaurant, his hand withdrawing to leave her chilled. After parking the car, he turned to face her, his expression both soft and strong as steel. "Marissa," he said slowly, reaching to twine a curl around his finger. "I don't know what's going on in your mind, but I want us to be married as soon as possible. If you have any reservations about us, I'll try to be patient, but you need to talk to me about them. Don't hold them in, hoping they'll go away, because they won't."

"I know," she said, touching his cheek to reassure herself that he really was there and with her. She had wanted this for so long that it seemed almost impossible to believe she was living her own fantasy. It frightened her. Nothing this good could last.... "Just give me a little time to get used to the idea of 'us,' okay?"

He sighed ruefully, letting go of her hair. "All right. But I want my baby born with *my* name on that certificate."

She flinched; the fantasy bubble popped. "I know." She scooted out the door before he could protest. She forced herself to grin. "Let's get something to eat. I'm starved!"

The restaurant was understated but elegant; the dinner, delicious. Marissa had loved crepes ever since she was a teenager, and to be able to chose from fifteen different kinds was close to heaven. They lingered over coffee, relaxing with each other both in words and in silence. The black-garbed waiters hovered in the background, their beaming smiles apparently appreciating customers who loved their specialties.

Adam chuckled, leaning back in his chair, replete. "I've never eaten dinner so early so many days in a row," he finally confessed.

"It's good for you," Marissa teased, eyeing his strong, lean frame. "If you eat and then get a little exercise, you won't become overweight."

"Is that why you eat early?" His eyes drifted down her form and then back again, mirth creasing his features delightfully.

It was her turn to chuckle. "I eat early because I got in the habit of doing it when I was teaching. Most schools serve lunch around eleven, and by four in the afternoon I'm starved."

His eyes crinkled with a smile. "So it's more for survival than from a duty to be healthy."

She shrugged, an impish grin appearing on her face. "I'm afraid so."

"Well, Marissa Madison, soon to be Marissa Pierce, no more starving and no more worrying. I'll take care of your diet from now on." He gave a mock frown, just like a schoolteacher scolding a student.

"Oh, but—" She began only to be interrupted by a booming voice.

"I finally tracked you down, Son. I've left enough messages to choke that damned secretary of yours. Obviously she's not too efficient."

"Hello, Dad," Adam said calmly, leaning back in his chair. "I received your messages."

Marissa stared up at the dapper older man standing at the edge of their table. His full head of salt-and-pepper hair visibly shook with anger even though he was attempting to smile. "When were you planning to get back to me?"

"As soon as I had time."

"You have time for *her*, but you can't take the time to give your own father a phone call?" the older man exclaimed. "That's a hell of a comment on our relationship."

It wasn't the words the older man muttered that hurt, it was the look in his eyes: cold, dismissing, cutting. His look spoke of everything ugly and disgusting.

Marissa reached for her purse, her face flaming. Of course his father would know who she was and that she was carrying Adam's child. "Excuse me," she said quietly, standing and retreating toward the back of the restaurant despite Adam calling her name. She had to get away. Quickly.

The bathroom was small, just large enough for one person at a time, thank goodness. She locked the door with shaking fingers, then leaned against the wall and stared at the young woman in the large plate-glass mirror.

Humiliation was new to her. So far she had been sheltered from that particular pain because she saw only friends, people who knew her and understood that no matter what her circumstances, she was not wanton or fallen or worth less than a hello.

But in Adam's father's eyes she was an interloper, someone who was trying to insinuate herself into a rich man's life. And there wasn't a doubt in her mind that most of his friends would believe the same thing.

Tears trickled down her cheeks and for the first time since she became pregnant she could attest to the fact that these tears had nothing to do with her carrying a child.

The ring glistened in the mirror above the sink as she raised her hand to wipe away a tear. Adam's ring—one she never would have worn if she hadn't gotten pregnant.

She jumped when the knock on the door vibrated through the small room. "Marissa, open up," Adam demanded and she stared at the wood as if he would materialize right in front of her. "Marissa! Open this door now before I get the management to do it for me!"

She thought about resisting, but the idea died before it bore fruit. What was the use? He'd make good his threat, and she'd look like an idiot.

With fingers that weren't quite steady, she flipped the lock, but as her hand circled the knob, the door burst open.

Adam's face was dark with strain. He stepped into the small space and quickly closed the door behind him, leaning against the wood as he searched her face to silently judge the damage done. She tilted her chin, deliberately challenging his scrutiny, but her sniffing ruined the effect.

"My father's an ass."

Her eyes widened. That statement was the last thing she'd expected. His thumb gently wiped away a tear. Then another. He smiled sadly. "He is, so don't try to tell me I should respect the bas—man. He's worried about our relationship because he's afraid you'll close the bank."

"The bank?" What was he talking about?

He nodded. "I support him. He's scared that if I marry a woman without money of her own, he'll lose out."

She searched his face, but it was implacable. "No."

"Yes," he said, his voice laced with anger. "He tracked me down so I could pay some pressing debts for him. It seems he gambled and lost and the people who hold his IOUs want their money immediately."

"Oh, Adam," she moaned, feeling so much pity and love mixed together that she couldn't stop herself from slipping her arms under his suit coat and wrapping them around his middle. "I'm so sorry," she sniffed.

He chuckled and the sound rumbled delightfully against her ear. He pulled her closer. "If it brings you out of the bathroom, I'll tell the whole gory story," he teased, but his grip on her back tightened.

She lifted her head and looked up, loving the lines around his mouth when he smiled as he was smiling now. "I acted like an ass, too."

"Yes."

She tilted her head and thought for a moment, then said slowly, "Perhaps if we invited your father over for Thanksgiving dinner and he saw that I wasn't after your money..."

"Then we could get married with his permission and blessing?"

She nodded.

His tender smile disappeared. "I'm afraid it doesn't work like that, honey, much as I would like it to. My family isn't anything like yours. There's no cement of love holding us together as there obviously is in yours—there's just money; green glue."

"Maybe it's your outlook that's tainting it. He *is* your father, Adam." Who could not help but love Adam, especially his father!

"Is *your* outlook tainting *your* father's image, Marissa?" he asked, and the look in her eyes told him he had hit a very sore spot. "I'm sorry."

She rested her hand against his neck, her fingers trailing the strength of his jaw. "No, you're right. I've seldom thought of him since Garner came into our life and changed it all around. But you're right. Not everyone is born with an instinct for parenting—it's something responsible people train for. Another one of God's miracles that don't fall on all people."

The knock on the door startled them both. Adam reluctantly let Marissa go, and with laughter replacing the solemnity of just a few moments ago, they opened the door to face a dour, mink-draped woman who had apparently lost her patience long ago. "Well, isn't this ridiculous!" her brows were pinched together in disapproval. "Couldn't you and your—girlfriend—have found a motel to fool around in, young man?"

"What a great idea," he murmured as he led Marissa around the woman's square form. "I'm surprised you know about them."

After Adam paid the bill and they walked outside, they both burst out laughing. It was a great way to end the day and make way for the evening.

CHRISTMAS SONGS and decorations began popping up the week before Thanksgiving. Every store pushed their wares as early and quickly as possible, hoping to lure customers into spending more than they had set aside for the holidays.

Marissa marched a cart up and down the grocery store aisles, humming along with the canned holiday music, examining the packages and containers as if she were on the tightest budget, when in fact Adam had insisted on paying for Thanksgiving dinner. Her contribution was the cooking.

She turned the aisle and stared at the shelves. Disposable diapers of every brand lined one side, their different sizes still a mystery she was trying to fathom. Other mothers, their baskets already filled with groceries and children, read labels and reached for their choices.

On the other side were the baby foods, also mysterious but something she was anxious to learn about. She'd been reading child-care manuals for months, and brand names along with nutritional guidelines were buzzing around her head like a swarm of bees.

"If you're trying to decide on cereal, you should also try the instant oatmeals," volunteered one mother with a smile.

"Does it work as well?"

The woman nodded. "But you have to use more hot water. When Kenny was small I ran out of his brand so I had to use his older brother's instant. It was fine."

Marissa smiled. "I'll remember that," she promised, backing her cart out to circle around the area. There was time enough for that later. Right now a Thanksgiving menu was what she ought to be worried about.

"When's the baby due?" continued the mother, pointedly staring at her stomach.

"Just before the New Year." Her hand covered the front of her shirt protectively, a smile on her lips.

"Your first?"

Marissa nodded.

The other woman chuckled. "Well, good luck. The first three years are the best, so they say. My husband, Jim, wonders now what it would have been like to be childless when he comes home and still has to start work all over again to repair what my boys destroyed that day."

"And you?" Marissa couldn't help asking, looking at the small eight- or nine-month-old baby in the shopping-cart seat. His hand was clamped proprietarily around a mushed cookie; his semitoothless smile was as bright as a new dime.

The woman sighed, reaching for a tissue to wipe the child's mouth. "Call me crazy, but I wouldn't have it any other way."

"I didn't think so." Marissa smiled, thinking that a mother's mannerisms might sometimes speak of anger or frustration, but the love in her eyes was a dead giveaway.

"You'll see," advised the other woman in a voice filled with warning and laughter. "We just don't get paid enough for the job we do. I figure about a million a year would be fair."

"All you have to do is find someone to pay it!"

The mother's eyes trailed down to the ring on Marissa's hand. "Looks like you found him already," she said dryly, finally setting the baby to rights in her cart. "Happy family," she blessed, wheeling slowly down the aisle, a smile on her face as she answered another child's question about different kinds of ice cream.

Groceries bought, Marissa drove into the underground parking and began unloading the bags. "Wait, Miss Madison!" the guard called. "I just called to the desk and Pete's on his way down to help."

For once she didn't mind. The entire back seat and trunk were filled. "Thanks," she called just as the elevator opened and both Pete and Adam stepped out.

Adam's hair was wet, his knit shirt clinging to his torso like a second skin. Faded jeans didn't detract from his slender hips and long legs—they emphasized. He looked fabulous. No matter what the man wore, he commanded attention.

He grinned when he saw the bags sitting across the back seat in a double line. "Buy out the store?"

"No, I left some for the rest of the world. Just barely."

She wanted to stretch up and kiss his cheek, smell the after-shave he wore, touch the muscles covering his arms and chest. But not with two of his employees standing there gawking and grinning.

It was as if he could read her mind, and his own smile and the slow-burning light in his gray eyes fueled her own desires.

Pete got one of the large luggage carriers and he and Adam stacked the groceries on it, but only after Adam had warned her to stand to one side.

"Men's work," she muttered under her breath, but was heard anyway.

"Correction. Sharing the load. You buy, I carry."

The giggle that rose in her throat couldn't be contained. "Like, me Tarzan, you Jane?" Although she had thought of him in a million different ways, she had never thought of him as a male chauvinist before.

"I'll handle that quip later," he warned ominously, but the glint in his eye made her catch her breath. If the weapon he used was what she hoped it would be, his retribution would be worth looking forward to.

"Yes, sir," she murmured obediently, following both men into the elevator.

They weren't in the apartment five minutes before the intercom buzzed. With muttered words under his breath and a can of pineapple in his hand, Adam strode into the hallway to answer it.

Marissa continued to hum a Christmas tune as she organized the groceries on the shelves and in the refrigerator.

It must have been the combination of talking to the woman in the store about children and having Adam help her with the job of storing groceries, but she suddenly saw herself as a wife and mother. Adam's wife. Motherhood she had gotten used to in the past few months, but the cloak of being a wife was still new and frightening—one she hadn't wanted to don until now.

Now she knew that life without coming home to Adam and her child could be the loneliest kind of life there is.

When Adam returned, Marissa wrapped her arms around his neck and kissed his cheek. "Everything all right?"

"Fine," he growled, his arms closing around her until she almost hurt. He took a deep breath and she could feel his chest expand. Then, slowly, he had to let it out. "But I've got a visitor," he said as he pulled back and stared down at her upturned face. "Can you handle this job alone?"

She tapped her chin as if thinking. "Gee, I don't know, it's just so overwhelming," she drawled in her best Scarlett O'Hara voice.

His smile didn't reach his eyes. He kissed the tip of her nose. "I'll be back in about an hour. Don't cook—I've got Italian food on the way."

"It's a waste when I've got all this." She stretched out an arm and waved toward the bags piled neatly on the countertops and floor.

"Don't cook." It was definitely an order.

Then he was gone, the can of pineapple still in his hand. Marissa began unpacking the nearest bag, her brow wrinkled in a frown. Whatever his visitor wanted, it had to be pressing business for him to forget what he was holding....

THANKSGIVING DAY DAWNED bright and shining, with the temperature in the midsixties.

Adam had spent the previous night in his own apartment, coming down only for dinner and then disappearing again under the guise of business. She chalked it up to the meeting he'd had with someone named Harrigan in Dallas, a name and a deal he had told her about not long ago.

Dressed in maternity pants and a bright azure over-size sweater, she began the preparations for the turkey and stuffings. Adam's dad was coming—grudgingly— for dinner and Marissa couldn't have been happier. Adam didn't seem to care one way or the other. She might not win the elder Mr. Pierce over, but at least she could tell herself that she had tried. After all, Adam had very little to do with the man on a personal level. As far as she knew, they only saw each other once or twice a month, and those meetings were held at the office in-stead of Adam's home.

Turkey and dressings in the oven, potatoes cut and in cold water on the stove, vegetables waiting for the microwave—she checked each item, wanting to do as little of the preparation as possible after Adam and his father arrived.

Freshly made yeast rolls sat on a baker's pan on the counter, alongside cranberry bread, carrot cake and the required pumpkin pie. Everything was as ready as she could make it.

Checking her appearance in the mirror while she nervously awaited them, she groaned. Her doctor had been concerned about her lack of weight gain. She was supposed to have added an extra eighteen pounds by now, yet she had only gained a little less than twelve and was in her eighth month. She was trying to gain more, but to her, the woman in the mirror didn't look as if she needed more. Why did she have to look like a blimp in the Macy's parade? From the chest up, she looked great, but she couldn't walk around with a bar-rel hiding the rest of her.

Sucking in her stomach, she stared again. Now her cheeks puffed out like a balloon fish and her face was turning an unbecoming shade of red. Her breath whooshed. It was no use. She was eight months pregnant and there was no denying it when it was as obvious as the nose on her face.

She turned away and sat on the couch, her emotions seesawing back and forth. No matter what she felt about herself, Adam had said over and over again that she wasn't ugly or fat or anything except beautiful. And it must be so, because she still saw that glint in his eye that told her he wanted her.

Only her own clumsiness made her feel so awkward; it was hard to pick up anything off the floor, tie her tennis shoes or clean the bathtub. All those things pointed to her changing body. She wasn't as self-assured as she used to be, but then she'd never been pregnant before, either.

And he had told her he loved her; he wanted to marry her. *She* was the problem—not Adam, not her looks, not their baby. And not his father.

She was ready, now, to voice a commitment to him. Perhaps later that night, after his father left and they were curled up in front of the fireplace with a glass of wine, replete from her cooking, she'd explain why she had been so hesitant to relinquish her freedom to him, and how she had been wrong.

A small smile curved her lips as she thought of the scene and how it would end.

They had been so happy together during the past few months—sharing, loving, laughing. So very happy. . .

The doorbell rang and she jumped. They were here! Briskly, she walked to the door. Her first holiday meal with her husband-to-be and his father was about to begin.

But when she opened the door, her heart sank to her feet. Neither man looked pleased. Adam's lips were pressed to a thin line, his brows deeply furrowed and his eyes the color of frozen snow at twilight. His father's chin was tilted up, as if he were trying to keep his nose in higher air so he wouldn't have to inhale the scent of a commoner.

She took a deep breath and pasted a smile on her face, determined to make the best of the situation. "Welcome," she said, standing aside so they could enter. "Won't you come in?"

"Hi, honey," Adam said quietly after following his father into the living room. He bent down and brushed a kiss across her cheek, his hand on her shoulder giving a light squeeze. But the preoccupied look in his eyes showed that he was only going through the motions.

She tried to ignore the thunder of her heart knelling doom and smiling again, walked toward the small side table she had set up as a bar. "Would you care for a drink, Mr. Pierce? Adam?"

"I'll fix them." Adam moved to the table and took her place. "You go ahead and do whatever you have to do." His voice was cool, reserved.

She looked from Adam to his father who was standing at the large patio door and looking out, his back stiff with . . . what? Anger? Tension? She couldn't tell. The only explanation was that they must have had an argument and it could have been over anything. The one thing she had learned recently was that they hardly ever saw eye-to-eye.

Silently she walked into the kitchen and fiddled with the burners. One look at the turkey told her dinner could be delivered to the table in less than an hour. Thank goodness. She didn't know if she could survive an afternoon of cold war. A small bubble of optimism told her that things could get better. Perhaps his father would realize she wasn't going to attack him or face his negative attitude head-on and he'd begin to relax.

An hour later, Marissa was kicking herself for living in a Pollyanna world. The situation hadn't gotten better; it was worse. Adam's father wasn't as much of a problem as Adam was. She wanted to comfort him—to be comforted by him—but he was too preoccupied for her to risk being rebuffed. So she kept a smile on her face while the heaviness in her heart kept gaining weight.

"More corn?" she asked brightly, holding up the bowl.

"No, thanks," Adam muttered, biting into a piece of turkey. He'd played with that same slice all through the meal.

His father didn't acknowledge her at all. In fact, he hadn't said more than three words since he walked into her apartment. With the exception of a long, narrow-eyed look that seemed to be dissecting her into small bloody pieces, he was succeeding in making her believe she was invisible.

Suddenly and without warning, she was filled with an anger that couldn't be contained. Both men deserved more than her anger—they needed to be hung by their thumbs over a boiling caldron of salt water! Red flashed in front of her eyes for a moment and she had to shake her head to see the two men through that haze. She took a deep breath, barely containing the words that pressed against her tongue dying to be spewed forth. Her head buzzed with the effort of remaining silent.

But the last straw was when Adam's father reached for the corn, picking up the bowl she had just offered and helping himself to another spoonful.

She flattened her hands on the table. "That's it," she muttered, forcing herself to push back her chair and walk toward the kitchen—and away from the men— before she exploded into a thousand brittle shards.

She walked stiff-legged out of the room. When she reached the kitchen, she rolled her shoulder around the doorway and pressed her forehead against the wall, purposely breathing shallowly so she wouldn't hyperventilate.

"I told you to behave yourself," Adam grated.

"She's certainly not Liz," Adam's father's voice was laced with an I-told-you-so tone.

"Drop Liz."

"The turkey's too dry."

"Then don't eat it."

"Liz would have had it catered correctly. She *knows* how to hostess."

By his tone, Marissa knew Adam's teeth had to be clenched together. "I don't give a damn what Liz is or is not. I'm marrying Marissa, and nothing you can say or do will change that. Get used to it, Dad, along with the list I gave you earlier."

Marissa held her breath, the pain in her chest too strong to allow her to breathe. Liz! The woman Adam had lived with for three years. At least he hadn't defended Liz to his father. At least . . .

"You didn't seem to mind her company either yesterday or an hour or so ago, Son. In fact, you were laughing and smiling."

"That's enough, Dad."

"And when you kissed her, I could have sworn—"

"Enough!" A fist hammered the table.

But his father continued. "Does this little gal know you'll probably be divorcing her as soon as you can legitimize that baby you seem to want so much? Does she believe Elizabeth won't bother waiting for you?"

The pain flowed from Marissa's chest through to the rest of her body, turning her legs and arms into dead, leaden weights. Adam's father hadn't said a word in front of her, but his thoughts were clear the moment she stepped out of the room. And so were Adam's actions, if his father's word was anything to go by. The fact that Adam didn't retaliate verified his actions.

She forced herself to move, slowly, carefully, but with great determination, out of the kitchen and toward the dining-room table. She should have known better than to pin all her hopes on one man. One trapped man . . .

"You've done your worst, now. I suggest you leave before I throw you out," Adam stated coldly, his eyes shooting icicles at his father, his hands fists on the table.

But Marissa ignored both their reactions. Her hands gripped the dining-room chair she had sat in earlier, and her eyes blazed the message her tongue was delivering. "I want both of you to get out of here now. Right this minute. And I don't want either of you to return. Ever." Her eyes rested meaningfully on Adam and his father.

Adam's expression was one of pain. But his father's showed the triumph he obviously felt. Realizing he had said exactly what he wanted her to overhear didn't matter—getting them out of her home was imperative. She took a deep, shuddering breath. "I said *now*," she gritted. "Go before I pour scalding water in your hot little laps."

Adam stood, leaning toward her. "Marissa," he began.

She held up her hand to ward off his words. "I don't want to hear it. Get out, Adam. Now."

He must have realized the strain she was under, the fact that all her blood had rushed to her feet, making them feel like hundred-pound weights. He hesitated a moment, then reached out to tuck a stray curl behind her ear.

"Don't touch me!" she cried, jerking away and almost losing her balance in the process. She grabbed at the table and steadied herself, her face even whiter than before. "Now get out, both of you." Her voice was barely above a whisper.

But both men heard her. Adam's father stood, placing his napkin next to his plate, and sauntered to the door.

Adam's face was stormy. "We'll talk about this later. As soon as I get rid of that dammed man who professes to call himself father."

"No. It's over." She pulled the diamond from her finger and held it out. Her chin tilted and she stared at him with eyes as blank as a black hole. "Goodbye."

He stared at the ring, his lips thinning. "I won't take it, Marissa. You and I aren't finished by a long shot." He turned his back on her and took the path his father had. "I'll be back in a few minutes."

Anger once more rose to block her sight. "Damn you, Adam Pierce!" she screamed and threw the ring at his back, hitting him just below the neck. He stopped for a split second, then continued toward the door, not even bothering to look at her, to curse her for her anger, to soothe away the hurt that seemed to be rooted in the very depths of her soul.

With the muted click of the door closing, Marissa lost the strength she had been clinging to so precariously. Her legs buckled and she dropped to the floor. Tears that had been held at bay by anger now fell, running down her cheeks until it seemed like a stream—one tear indistinguishable from another.

With sobs caught in her throat, she leaned her head forward to rest on her arms.

She closed her eyes, a prayer drifting through her mind. But it was too late for prayers. She was alone again and would have to face the future knowing that it was the only way she could continue.

The interlude of daydreams and true love was over. Reality had descended with a crash. Loneliness was just around the corner, waiting for her like an old nemesis. But at least she knew what to expect in the future—all she had to do was get used to it. Again.

10

ADAM'S HANDS were clenched into fists. He stepped into the elevator and stood facing the front, unable even to look at his father. "You're leaving for good," he ordered softly through gritted teeth. "You're getting out of this building and out of my life. Right now."

"Wait a minute, Son. Your little girlfriend was bound to find out sooner or later that Liz is still in the picture."

"Liz is dead as far as I'm concerned. You knew that, but you chose to use Liz as a weapon. Bad choice."

"She didn't seem dead when you were kissing her this afternoon."

"Wrong," Adam gritted. "She kissed me. I pushed her away. Liz and I have nothing to do with each other. You knew that, but you used it to try to manipulate me. Now it's over."

"But why?" His father grabbed his arm. "Why, when she has almost as much money as you do? She likes the same things, knows the same people! She even wants to have your baby."

Adam shrugged off his father's hand, unable to conceal the shudder of disgust that flowed through him.

"Adam, listen to me," the older man said quickly. "You could marry Liz, and if this little girl means so much to you, you could still see her. After all, you're paying for her apartment. You're paying for everything's she's got!"

His father's words slammed into him like a battering ram; he was right. Adam had taken Marissa's independence away from her and forced her to rely on him, only to throw her trust and love back in her face by the way he'd acted today. He had only taken from Marissa, never given anything but money. He'd been acting like an image of his father—doing the very things he had detested all his growing years.

Ever since he could remember, his father had given money to his mother and himself in place of the love they had craved. At times he hadn't even given them that. And Adam had done just the same thing to Marissa. He had backed her against a wall, leaving her no escape—and then deserted her.

She loved him. He knew that now. She loved him enough to give up her independence for him and had proven it over and over again in the past months. But she was still frightened; he saw it in her eyes when she wasn't aware he was looking. But she was so brave, willing to show her love and willing to put her love on the line.

His heart fluttered anxiously. He had to get back to her and explain. In so many ways she was much wiser than he.

He turned eyes that were as cold as an Arctic storm on his father. "The bills you delivered this afternoon are the last bills I'll ever pay. You want to spend money, you'd better earn it. And the rest of the rules and regulations we discussed will be followed. No more gambling, no more throwing women in my way, no more anything from you—including arguments like we had before we got to Marissa's door, or snide remarks like those you just threw out. We're through."

The elevator stopped at the ground floor and the doors opened. Adam stood stiffly, his eyes straight ahead. "Goodbye."

"Son, let me . . ."

"Goodbye."

His father's shoulders slumped as he stepped off, turning once more to his son. The elevator doors closed and Adam punched the button for Marissa's floor. He had to get to her, see her, talk with her and convince her of his love. His anger with his father had spilled over into Marissa's living room. He could hardly speak to the man, let alone eat in his presence or share a holiday he had wanted to be perfect and spent just with Marissa.

Adam hadn't wanted his father there and had partially blamed Marissa for his being thrown together with him. They had just had a knock-down-drag-out fight about the older man's life-style, and Adam should have known that he was more than capable of getting even for that. Instead, Adam had tempted the Fates by allowing his father access to Marissa so he could hurt her. That bit about Elizabeth had been brought up cold-bloodedly and on purpose—something his father wanted Marissa to hear but that had no basis in fact. She had to believe Adam. She had to!

The unbearable pain that had shone from her eyes haunted him. Damn his father! As soon as the elevator stopped at her floor, impatient steps took him quickly to her apartment door. But his knock and ringing of the doorbell brought no answer. Finally he fumbled for the key.

Was she hurt? Had that debacle of a Thanksgiving harmed the baby? He said a quick prayer as he opened the door and called her name.

The table was still laden with the remnants of dinner, the kitchen counter filled with unwashed dishes. He knew housekeeping idiosyncrasies wouldn't allow her to leave it for long. He called again. "Marissa? Where are you?"

He strode to the baby's room and glanced in. She had hung the decorations on the wall over the past few days. The room looked as if it were expecting a child. His child.

He shortcut through the bathroom to her bedroom, then stopped in the center of the room. Clothing was pulled out of the closets, shoes lay scattered on the floor. Her makeup was gone. "Dear God, no!" he groaned.

Then he ran toward the front door and the elevators, only to spot something glinting on the floor. Stooping, he picked it up and stared at the ring in his palm. Marissa's ring. Everything it stood for flashed through his mind. Her loving care, her smile, her winsome ways. Her love. Their baby. The happiness he'd naively thought was his. Tears made the stone glisten even more.

With it clenched tightly in his hand, he strode down the hallway and stepped into the first open elevator. She must have taken an elevator down while he was returning to her apartment in another. He had to catch her. She couldn't leave feeling that he had lied to her. She had to know how much he loved her.

The elevator took its sweet time descending and he wanted to scream at the slowness of it. When it finally opened to the garage, he rushed out, only to stand still again. Her car was gone, the slot empty.

He wanted to scream out his pain, yell at the gods for tricking him into silence when he should have been vocal. He wanted the horrible emptiness in his soul to be filled. With Marissa. With his child.

Running on instinct and anguish, he turned and hit the cinder-block wall with his fist, and the pain of it ran through his brain, blocking out the emptiness for just a moment. Calmly and with deliberation, he wrapped his fist in his handkerchief and walked to his car.

He was going to find Marissa and bring her back. Whether she wanted to live with him or without him, she would live here—in his building, under his care. He would give her back her freedom, allow her to do whatever she wanted without his interference.

It was the only thing he had left to offer, for he knew she'd spurn him otherwise. The agony of losing what he loved and wanted most gave him no other alternative.

But first things first. He had to find her, and then he had to convince her that what he was going to say was also what he was going to do.

THE TWO WEEKS after Thanksgiving were the toughest Marissa had ever lived through. She'd thought that telling Adam about the baby was rough, but it had turned out to be child's play compared to the emotions she was experiencing now.

Every morning she awoke in Becca's apartment and stared at the ceiling, wondering how she was going to make it through the day. Every evening she went to bed knowing that she was going to dream of Adam and the happiness they had shared over the past few months. For just a little while she had pretended that he loved her and wanted both her and their child. But his lack of compassion when he was with his father, and his father's own words condemning his actions were enough to bring her to her senses. She should have known better, she silently kept berating herself.

She gave up her part-time job at the insurance company. Adam would hunt her down because he wanted his baby, and she couldn't let him find her. If she thought he could find her at Becca's, then she'd have to leave immediately and head for home and her parents. Instead, she prayed he'd give up the search and leave her alone to patch her life together as best she could.

During the day she drove to the various malls and walked the concourses, mingling with the milling Christmas-shopping crowds and getting the exercise the doctor had insisted she needed for natural childbirth. It was hard to breathe—the baby seemed to rest comfortably just over her lungs so that every few minutes she would have to stop and take a deep breath; then she'd continue to walk. Two nights a week she took Lamaze classes, readying herself for her child's birthday. It kept her mind occupied . . . for a little while.

She'd never noticed the sadness of the holiday season before. Mothers with small children barely under control frowned as they rushed through the stores looking for bargains that fit their budgets. Some would count their cash as if they were misers on a reluctant binge, while others would try to remember the limits on their credit cards. Then others, like herself, were alone and trying to fit into the gaiety of the season but with no success. Christmas was a lonely time without someone to share it with.

In the evenings she would walk the small hallway of Becca's apartment as her friend graded papers at the kitchen table. When the lateness of the hour curtailed that activity, she would prop herself in bed with pillows and begin the night the same way she ended it: replaying the past few months.

Tears were never far away. Neither was the sadness she wore like a hair shirt.

"You've got to stop this," Becca said, throwing the pencil down and glaring at her friend. "This isn't good for you or the baby. Especially the baby."

Marissa grinned, but the sadness was still there. "Don't use the baby as a weapon, Becca. The doctor said that walking was excellent exercise."

"Not if you do it until you've got bloody stumps for feet."

"I'm fine."

Becca pushed herself to standing. "The hell you are. You're a wreck and I'm not going to sit here and watch you ruin your health, both mental and physical, over a man."

Marissa forced an impassive expression. "I'm not a wreck. I'm pregnant and it's the Christmas season and I'm lonely for my family."

"You're lonely for Adam," Becca corrected, not allowing her friend to delude herself. "And he's a horse's behind for carrying on with you while carrying on with Liz."

"It was the other way around. Liz is the one who should be upset. Not me. She was in the picture long before he . . . noticed me." An unbelievable sadness touched her soul and she had to look away from Becca until she could control herself.

"Marissa, I ought to tell you, there was a man who was snooping around the school office yesterday. He said he was trying to find a teacher named Becca about an inheritance from her aunt. I don't have an aunt."

Marissa's head snapped up. "What did they tell him? Was it Adam?"

"I think it was a private detective, but Shirley, the office secretary, told them my last name and that they'd have to reach me by mailing a letter to the school. If I wanted to answer, then I would. They didn't give out my address."

Panic surged through her and she turned quickly, heading for her room. "I'm sorry Becca, and thanks, but I've got to go."

"Hey!" Becca exclaimed, but it was too late. Marissa was behind the closed door of her room, packing.

It took her a half hour to throw her things together—the longest time in the world. She cried the entire time, silently brushing away the tears that hindered her flight. It wasn't until she was through and sat on the bed, that she wondered what she was going to do next. Her parents. She'd take the next flight to Shreveport and stay with them.

She tried to convince herself that this whole nightmare would be over soon and then she could settle down to teaching and being a parent—only looking back at this time in her life to use as a yardstick to measure the confusion of her own tangled emotions. By then she'd be content with her life and only missing Adam occasionally. Time would take care of her heart. And if it didn't, she would manage anyway. After all, she had loved Adam from afar for three years and she still functioned during that time. She could do it again.

The knock on her door interrupted her reverie. She straightened and swiped at the tears on her cheeks. "Yes, Becca," she called tiredly.

But when the door opened, it was Adam who filled the frame. Adam whose gray eyes burned into hers. Adam whose anger roared through the air between them in giant waves that threatened to engulf her.

He glanced at the suitcases standing in the middle of the room. "Running again, Marissa? Haven't you caught on yet that I'll find you anywhere you go?"

She shrugged in lieu of words, unable to find her voice and tell him exactly where he could go.

"You believed my father's ramblings, didn't you?" His voice softened.

"Are you telling me he lied? That Liz wasn't in your apartment? That you weren't kissing? That you don't want custody of this child so badly you'd lie, cheat and steal?"

"No."

Her last thread of hope was gone. "Then we have nothing to discuss."

He crossed his arms and leaned against the door-jamb. His face was implacable. "Yes, we do. You're coming back with me and we'll work this out. Together."

"Read my lips, Pierce: N-O." Her brown eyes blazed with golden shards of glass she prayed would shred his soul.

He closed his eyes a moment and silence hung in the air. When he opened them again, they were aimed toward her, shining with determination. "If you come back and listen to my explanation, I promise I'll abide by your decision if you decide to leave me again."

"How generous!" she sneered, ruining it with a sniff. "But you don't own me. I can do that now."

"No, you can't. I'll follow you wherever you go, haunting you until you give me equal time. But you have to be fair. I promise I'll never interfere again if you'll just listen to me."

"No!"

He continued as if she hadn't spoken. "But if you're not fair, don't expect me to be, either. I'll play dirty if I have to. I'll file the biggest lawsuit you've ever seen and win custody of our child," he stated softly. "I can do it— and you know it."

Her heart sank. Something in the back of her mind told her that he wouldn't do what he was threatening, but was she willing to take that chance? "We'll talk here," she said belligerently.

"No."

All the breath—and spark—went out of her. "All right, Adam. You win. This time," she added, standing to reach for one of her suitcases. "But when our little talk is over, I want to be able to leave immediately."

"Of course." His bland expression should have alarmed Marissa even more, but she was too numb to pay more than cursory attention to it. He strode into the room and began gathering the luggage. "Let's go."

Her goodbye to Becca was cause for more tears. Old friends were valued friends and never more than now when Marissa felt so alone.

The car ride back to the tower was quiet. Neither said a word, but the tension that was locked inside the car was more frightening than anything she had experienced before.

It wasn't until they entered her apartment that she came out of the fog that seemed wrapped around her brain. Glancing at the polished dining table, she asked the first thing that popped in her mind. "Who cleaned?"

"I did." Adam set the suitcases against the wall, then stood with hands on his hips as if daring her to say anything.

She didn't. Taking a seat in the rocker, she continued the silence she had maintained until then. Her head drifted back and her eyes closed in weariness. She must have dozed off because the next thing she knew, Adam's after-shave wafted in the air and the brush of a kiss whisked against her cheek.

Her lashes fluttered, then opened, to stare at Adam. Her heart sang with joy at the loving expression on his face—until she remembered the series of events that her sleeping mind had chosen to forget for a few moments.

"I love you, Marissa."

She closed her eyes and swallowed. "You have a perverted sense of humor."

"I have no humor at all without you. You're the fun and life and joy I need."

She forced herself to answer. "And what's Liz? The beautiful habit?"

"Liz was a live-in for three years and, yes, she was a beautiful habit. One I didn't love. We parted as friends, and we're still friends. But we're not lovers and we haven't been since a week before the night I spent with you. She's also one of the most savvy real-estate minds in the business and I had a business deal she was working on."

"How convenient for you." Marissa's voice was syrupy sweet.

He ignored her sarcasm. "The night before Thanksgiving she received a confirmed price on a piece of property that she knew I was interested in. She tried to contact me at work but Judi didn't tell me, thinking it was personal. Finally, she called my dad and he brought her to my apartment. We confirmed the prices and she gave me a celebratory kiss on the cheek when she left."

"Of course," Marissa choked. Why was he doing this to her? "That explains why you were so cold and rude. You were thrilled to death with a real-estate deal."

He ran a hand around his neck and gave a deep sigh. "No, I was mad at you for insisting I invite my father to a holiday I didn't want to celebrate with him. To top it all off, he and I had a knock-down-drag-out fight just before we walked in. He said what he did to get back at me. And you bought it." He ran a hand around his neck, easing the tense muscles. "Not everyone has the fathering instinct, Marissa. You ought to know that."

She was confused and upset enough without listening to more, and she was still unable to tell truth from fiction. Standing, she stepped around him and walked toward the kitchen, bargaining for time by pretending to drink a glass of water.

"Marissa."

The glass halted halfway to her lips.

"My father was lying. I have no intention of leaving you. Now or ever." He walked toward her, not stopping until he was close enough to touch her. "Stay. Let me prove to you that I love you." His voice was a harsh whisper in the quiet.

She turned and carefully placed the glass on the counter and leaned with a hand on each side of the sink, staring at the garbage disposal as if it held answers for her. "No, Adam. We've had plenty of time to see if this would work. It didn't."

He rested his hands on her shoulders, giving a light squeeze. She wished with all her might that she had the nerve to lean back on the strength of his chest. Just for a moment.

"Please. After the baby is born, if you decide to leave, I'll understand." His grip tightened to massage the tightness out of her slim shoulders, but he could feel her tense even more. His hands stilled. "Your doctor is here, the date for the baby's delivery is less than a month off, and everything is arranged."

Tears pressed against her eyelids. Adam was pleading, asking her to stay, but she knew, deep down, that it would never work. She sighed. "All right. Until the baby is born. Under two conditions."

She could feel him relax, then stiffen. "What?"

"That you no longer use my home as a second home. And that you sign an agreement to leave both me and my child alone after the New Year."

Silence stretched between them. Marissa continued to stare straight ahead as she waited for his decision. Either way, she would be free. Either way she would be alone....

"I agree." He expelled his breath and the warmth of it touched her neck and the side of her cheek like a caress. "You won't be sorry. I promise."

"Fine. Now please leave." She couldn't take his nearness anymore. Suddenly she was as exhausted as if she had run a marathon. And her muscles hurt—everywhere.

"I..." he began, then the silence descended again. They stood as two statues, back to front, and neither wanted to move. "All right," he said slowly, his voice a mere whisper. "I'll leave for now, but I get to check up on you from time to time."

She nodded, too weary to argue. "After every doctor's visit on Tuesdays. I'll keep you informed then."

He lifted his hands and walked away, leaving her cold and alone, bending over a sink when she wanted to be enclosed in his arms, being told he loved her with a fervor that would convince her. But she knew better than to play those let's-pretend games anymore. She'd learned the hard way.

The door clicked hollowly as he walked out. And with him went the anger and frustration of the past weeks. All that was left was an aching loneliness that permeated the walls of the apartment, the furniture, her.

She shuffled toward the bedroom. She'd call Becca later. In fact, she'd do everything else that needed doing later. Right now she needed sleep.

It was almost noon the next day when she awoke. Stretching, she smiled. She hadn't felt this good and energetic in years! She patted her stomach, idly wondering if this was the burst of energy that some women get just before delivery. A few books called it the nesting syndrome, explaining that it led to a cleaning and purging of the house before the baby arrived. A glance at the calendar told her differently: she still had two full weeks to go.

She fixed decaffeinated coffee, then her eyes narrowed as she saw her handwriting in today's square. December eighteenth. Tuesday. She had an appointment with the doctor in exactly one hour.

The light came on and she filled a cup with the brew before she strolled into the living room and looked around as if seeing it for the first time. This was Christmas and she didn't have one decoration to celebrate the season!

Energy filled her to overflowing as she rushed her shower and dried her hair, slipping into her blue maternity dress with the red bow at the throat. She'd moped around for over two weeks doing nothing but feeling sorry for herself. Well it was about time for a change.

Adam or no Adam, Christmas was here and she was going to do something about it. The baby gave a mighty kick as if to agree.

The doctor confirmed what Marissa already knew: the baby hadn't budged from its position. Just in case everything wasn't as ready as the physician had expected, an ultrasound was requested. It was the closest thing to a miracle that Marissa had ever seen.

With her doctor beside her, she was perched on a table so her head tilted up, then the nurse smeared her stomach with a gooey substance. A small portable machine with a four-inch screen was wheeled to her side and a probe slid across her belly.

Wide-eyed, Marissa watched the technician. On the screen appeared the perfect vision of an infant. "Is that the baby?" she whispered, awed.

"Yup," the technician chuckled. "Do you want to see if we can find out its sex?"

"Can you?"

"We can try."

Marissa stared at the picture in wonder. It was her baby, perfectly formed. "Yes, please," she finally whispered.

The technician switched the instrument's angle, forming more pictures as she went. With another chuckle, she pushed a button and out came a Polaroid of the image. "She's a little beauty, isn't she? I'd say about seven pounds and maybe twenty inches long. She's in position and ready to drop for the big delivery day."

"She?"

The woman nodded, her eyes still glued to the screen. "I'd say ninety-nine percent sure. It's a perfectly clear picture and that's indoor plumbing. Besides, she's much too pretty to be a snakes-and-toads boy, wouldn't you say?"

Marissa laughed, the bubbling sound wondrous. "She. I'm having a she!"

"Now you can buy all the pink you want."

"I'm having a she!"

"This time," the technician warned. "Remember you have a fifty-fifty chance with each baby. Maybe next time it'll be a boy."

The smile left her mouth but not her eyes. They sparkled. "I don't care about the next time. I'm concerned with this one."

"And it looks as if a New Year's delivery date might be right on target unless she drops more in the next few days."

But Marissa didn't care about the details. God had heard her prayers and that was all that mattered. Two more Polaroids were taken and torn off the machine, then handed to her. She couldn't take her eyes off them the entire time she dressed. It was her baby daughter's first picture. The baby she had dreamed of for over eight months was real and these pictures proved it.

When she left the office with more directions on diet and exercise, she was walking on air—even with her size.

Suddenly the songs wishing everyone a Merry Christmas or telling of roasting chestnuts on an open fire added to her buoyancy. She walked the mall with a lightness in her heart she hadn't felt in ages.

After filling the car with gifts, wrapping paper, tape and boxes, she headed to the nearest tree lot, picking the best-looking five-foot tree she could find. It was so bushy and fresh, it was guaranteed to fill the apartment with the scent of pine.

The last stop was the grocery store, where she bought the ingredients for several kinds of cookies and breads. What was Christmas without the frills? Underlying her happiness was a small kernel of sorrow for spending the holiday alone, but she replaced that thought with another: next year she would have her daughter to care for and love.

Dusk was just descending when she reached the parking garage and called for help from the lobby. The lightness of her step and the sparkle in her eyes must have been catching, for Peter cracked Christmas jokes while enjoying her laughter all the way to her door.

ADAM GLARED at the sunset from the brisk chilliness of his patio where he stood, drink in hand. Then he began what had been a ritual lately: pacing the concrete. Where had Marissa spent the day? She'd had a doctor's appointment early this afternoon and hadn't returned until five minutes ago. He knew because the downstairs desk had told him.

He wanted to go to her and demand an explanation, but he didn't have the nerve. Afraid of losing her again, he had found his own Achilles' heel, his own weakness: Marissa's emotions. She now managed to affect his whole way of thinking, doing, living.

And deep down in his gut, there was an overwhelming ache for her that couldn't be assuaged unless he was close to her, privileged to see her smile tilt the delicious corners of her mouth, to bask in the dancing golden light of her eyes, to be warmed by her love of life and joy in living.

He had almost snuffed out that light once, and he couldn't take the chance of losing it again. So instead, he stood on a cold patio and stared down at the Christmas lights of the city and mooned over his plight.

What did she want from him that he wasn't giving her? He had declared his love for both her and the baby, believing she would recognize it as truth. He had explained the actions of both himself and his father as honestly as he could. The only thing he hadn't mentioned was the deal that Liz was working on, which was to be a Christmas present for Marissa. He had tried as hard and as earnestly as possible to show her how deep his love for her ran.

He stopped pacing, narrowing his eyes to stare into the gray night. He wasn't the problem. He grinned, then chuckled aloud. *He wasn't the problem!*

Why hadn't he seen it before? Marissa was the product of a forced marriage and must have suffered greatly from that experience, carrying emotional scars that he couldn't even dream of. She had had a father who continued to blame both her mother and her for ruining his chances at life, and then left them to fend for themselves. Adam would have bet on the probability that as a child she had craved her father's affection and approval. But she hadn't gotten them, and now she was more than frightened to put herself in such a position again. So frightened that she refused to believe her own emotions—let alone his.

He remembered the night they had made love and conceived the child. She had given herself to him with no reservations then, opening herself as she had probably never done before, only to have him walk out the door and out of her life, which only reinforced her earlier beliefs.

"Damn!" he muttered, mentally kicking himself for running away from her. Then she had been poison to him, a weight of commitment that scared the hell out of him. But that had changed. *He* had changed. Amazing that he had thought he had grown up all those years ago, only to find that growing up was a continuous process—and hard as hell.

But he'd done a lot of growing lately, and he knew what he wanted now. All he had to do was to prove to Marissa that he'd never let her down again. Never.

He glanced at his watch. He'd wait an hour or two and then he'd casually stroll down to her place and ask what the doctor had to say. He'd put no pressure on her and maybe, with a little space for her to breathe, she'd see him as the man she'd been waiting for all her life.

If that didn't work, he'd kiss her until she couldn't see straight!

As Oh Holy Night played on the radio, he offered a prayer that his hopes for a miracle and just a little magic weren't in vain.

11

MARISSA HUMMED Christmas songs as she mixed gingerbread batter. Intent upon making nothing but little-girl cookies, she decided to ice them with pinks and reds and use raisins for eyes and mouths. Propped on the kitchen counter was one of the pictures of her daughter; she glanced at it every few minutes, patting her stomach and smiling with the bubbling happiness that welled inside her. A small circle of flour now covered that often-patted spot.

The tree was standing, brightly decorated, by the side of the fireplace. A fire one of the guards had built for her was crackling in the hearth. The smell of the first batch of cookies mingled with fresh-cut pine to fill the apartment with scents of Christmas. In a few minutes she'd sit down with her lemon-and-honey drink to enjoy her handiwork.

Earlier she had called Becca, and her friend had promised to visit later this evening. That was for her own protection. Sooner or later Adam would show up, and when he did she wasn't going to be alone with him. She glanced at her watch when the doorbell rang and went to the door. Eight o'clock. Becca was early. Wiping her hands on a dish towel, she opened her door, an impish smile on her face.

But instead of Becca, Adam stood there, his gray eyes compelling her to step back. She glanced at him warily. Having seen that look on his face before, she wondered what he was up to. She felt herself retreat from his very presence. That look usually meant a confrontation—with her on the defensive while he stalked his prey. "Well, hello, Mr. Pierce," she said sweetly, going for the bimbo routine.

"Hello, Miss Madison." His look encompassed her, a broad smile spanning his mouth and crinkling his eyes. "You look . . . housewifely."

She glanced down, for the first time seeing the large splash of flour on her front. Trying to wipe it away only made it worse and while she attacked the problem, he slipped through the doorway. Unless she wanted a scene, she had no choice but to accept his company. Besides, she thought as she gave in to his being there, she had promised he could see her after every visit to the doctor.

"Busy day?" he asked blandly.

"Very. Would you like a gingerbread girl?"

"I'd love one." *One in particular.*

He started to follow her to the kitchen, but the sight of the tree stopped him. He stared at it, then swallowed hard.

She glanced at him over her shoulder, then she stopped, too. For the first time she looked at her tree from a stranger's point of view. "I know it looks like a child's tree, but that's the way I like them." She hadn't meant that defensive tone to creep into her voice, but she couldn't help it.

"Are those cranberries? And popcorn?" he asked, his voice husky.

She nodded, still wary. "The paper chains were given to me by my students two years ago. Each student made one with their favorite topic of the week and signature written on it."

"It's a very special tree," he finally said.

She couldn't answer. It was true, but no one but her parents and Becca knew how special it was to her. Every ornament had a history behind it—even the most bedraggled ones. And all the stories involved one form of love or another—including the new ornament, a big silver ball with the name Taylor Jessica laced in gold sparkles. Her daughter's first ornament.

He walked closer to peer at the decorations, then looked at her a moment. "Taylor Jessica?"

She nodded.

"You seem awfully sure you're going to have a girl."

She couldn't help the giggle that burst forth. "I *am* sure." Ducking into the kitchen, she plucked the picture off the counter and walked to his side. "Would you like to see our daughter?" she asked softly.

He accepted the photo, but didn't look at it right away. Instead he searched her face—for what? But his slow smile took the edge off her wariness. She knew he was touched by the decorations, but then again, since he was a bachelor, he probably didn't have a strong urge to celebrate the season by himself.

Then he looked at the picture in his hand. "My God," he whispered. "How did they do that? It's a perfect photo!"

She chuckled, looking over his arm. "I know, isn't it a miracle? They do it by soundwaves. Isn't she adorable? Her little hand is over her heart, as if she's making a pledge."

His eyes never left the picture. "But how do you know it's a girl?"

Marissa laughed aloud. "The usual way, Adam."

"You mean . . . ?" He glanced at her, then back at the photo. A blush crept up his neck.

She nodded.

"Are they sure?"

She nodded again. "Ninety-nine percent sure."

Taking a step back, he plopped on the couch, the picture in front of him. "A baby girl named Taylor Jessica," he murmured, as if saying it would make it more real.

She walked toward the kitchen, leaving him alone to adjust to the news that hadn't really soaked into her own head. Fixing coffee was done automatically. Then, placing newly baked cookies on a small plate, she walked back into the living room.

Adam was still staring at the photo, but now his hand shook as he looked up at her. "Marissa—" he cleared his throat "—Marissa, this is *my* child and I want to help raise her. She's a part of me and a part of you, what could possibly be more magical than that?"

That sadness that had been with her ever since she'd found out she was pregnant swamped her again. How could he ask her that when she was at her most vulnerable? It had only been recently that she had banished her black cloud of problems to the back of her mind. "Damn you, Adam Pierce."

He reached out and touched the side of her cheek, his fingers caressing her as if she were precious. "I've been damned since the moment I laid eyes on you, Marissa. I've needed and wanted and been cursed with those feelings until I can't remember when you weren't a part of my life."

She sat still, her eyes pinned by his. Then she shook her head, breaking the spell. "You'll remember soon enough," she said sadly but with conviction. "After Taylor is born and you find that fathering is more than playing with a little doll, the newness will wear off and you'll be back on your own track in life again. You'll have your father to worry about and Elizabeth to help you forget your worries."

His hand stilled. "I don't give a damn for Elizabeth and my father is gone for good. Besides, I'm not talking about playing with a baby. I want to be there when she takes her first step, speaks her first word, tumbles in her first fall, rides her first bike, and cries over her first boyfriend. I want the good and the bad and the loving."

"We'll see," she said, staring over his shoulder as she remembered another man who had never been around when his daughter needed him. Her own father was always one to talk about what he missed, but never one to do anything about it except moan. Most of the men she had run into were the same way—willing to brag, but disconnected from the joy and heartbreak of true commitment to their children.

"We're not going to see about anything. I was speaking of loving you and you twisted it around to our daughter—one who isn't born yet, I might add. But you've already condemned me to a role you've written and directed, and all without taking me or my feelings into account." His voice was filled with restrained anger. "I've let you get away with this long enough, and now it's time to put my foot down. You're marrying me on Christmas Day, Marissa, just like we planned. No ifs, ands or buts. I'll call your parents so they can come up for it. We'll have a small ceremony in my apartment."

"No."

"Yes." Steel couldn't have been harder than his voice. "If you won't, I'll have you watched until the baby is born. Then I'll file for custody." His smile was almost feral. "I have more money than you do. Who do you think will win?"

"You're blackmailing me." Her voice was a whisper, her throat closing off with every swallow. "You're doing it again."

He nodded slowly. "Yes. I've tried everything else."

"Don't," she said, pressing her hand against his chest in her attempt to plead with him. "Please."

"I'm sorry, darling, but I've done everything I can to convince you that I love you and want our child. It isn't me that's afraid of commitment, it's you. And the only way you'll get over this fear is to plunge into this marriage and find out for yourself that we were really meant to be together."

"You're crazy."

He smiled. "I was until now. I tried to give you enough rope to hang yourself with, but all you did was get tangled up in a bunch of emotions that don't have a damn thing to do with us. Now I'm taking over and we'll get this mess straightened out before our daughter is born. Maybe in fifteen or twenty years you'll understand just how much I love you and you'll accept me for what I am—a man who's crazy about his wife and children.''

She cleared her throat and wished she could clear her mind. It was reeling. "Children?"

"Of course," he said calmly. "We'll have more, I'm sure. You're too sweet and giving to settle for one. Besides, we're both only children and I'd make a guess neither of us enjoyed the experience. We wouldn't want to do the same to Taylor."

She rubbed her temple. "I'm insane and this isn't happening."

"We'll be married in a week, Marissa. No more skirting the issues. I'll make the arrangements," he said quietly. "And I promise I'll never do anything to hurt you. Not ever." He clasped her trembling hand and held it in both of his. "I love you, Marissa, and I think this is the only way I can prove it. And you love me, too. I know it."

"It won't work," she answered shakily.

"Yes, it will." He tilted her chin up with a finger. "But, honey, there aren't any guarantees in this world. We'll both have to work hard to make sure our marriage works. Nothing comes right without working at it."

Her hands fell to her lap and she stared out the patio window, unable to cope with his ultimatum. A sob caught in her throat. And she had thought she could handle him! That he wouldn't care whether he was having a child or not! It was all so damned funny! She had expected him to behave as her father had, running from a commitment when all he had wanted was a little fun. How wrong she had been. How very wrong . . .

Adam rose and passed in front of her without her even seeing him. She sat, continuing to stare out at the night sky as she grappled with her tumbling thoughts. The harder she sought a way out of the marriage, the more she knew she'd go through with it. She was tired of fending off the man she loved while she waited to be sure that it was herself he loved instead of the baby he felt responsible for. There really was no way for him to prove his love, so she either had to accept his word or slowly die of misery.

She knew she could still run away, but why? Everything she wanted was here, in Adam. And he was right: there were no guarantees—only hope and faith and trying to resolve whatever future problems would arise.

She had no choice.

"Marissa?" Adam's voice was soft as he knelt in front of her, taking her cold hands in his once more. He rubbed them between the warmth of his palms. "Are you okay?"

She nodded, finally leaning back and resting her head on the edge of the sofa. "You win, Adam. I can't fight anymore."

He squeezed her hands. "I know."

She sighed, losing her own battle and suddenly feeling as if a weight had fallen from her shoulders. "What will your father and Liz say?"

She could feel him stiffen. "This has nothing to do with them. After this week I doubt if we'll ever see either of them again."

"Will you continue to see her after we're married?"

"No."

She believed him. Was she still playing the fool? She didn't now.

"Becca came by and said she'd call you later," Adam said, interrupting her reverie. Her head seemed to be wrapped in cotton. She nodded. Just thinking of talking to Becca was too much of an effort.

Adam sat down on the couch and pulled her, unresisting, into his arms. Suddenly his strength was a deep comfort. No more fighting, no attempting to remain her own person separate from his almost overwhelming personality, no more doubts about his need of her. Perhaps, in time, he'd come to love her as she needed to be loved. Oh, he had said the words right now, but it was only to get his own way, she knew. The baby was his objective and God help anyone who got in the way of Adam's prime target.

She sighed and closed her eyes, flowing with the drifting of his breathing until she was asleep in his arms.

Adam stared at the tiny, feminine hand he held in his own, searching for a way to prove his love for her. His mind was a blank. Until she had shown him that photo of their baby he had had no reason to push her into a corner like that. But it wasn't until then that he realized there was no reasoning with a woman who was as strong-headed as his Marissa was. She would fight to the end or until she realized the battle was over. And it was definitely over. He could no more let her go than he could stop breathing.

His arms tightened. Christmas was just seven days away. Seven long days. And somehow he'd have to prove in that short time that she was the woman of his dreams.

Marissa shifted against him and the immediate response his body gave told him just what a louse he was. He wanted her—heavy with his child, exhausted by her efforts at putting him off—he still wanted her.

One hand cupped her enlarged stomach protectively as he reminded himself of their child's presence. That was no way for his daughter to get to know her father. He leaned his head back and willed his body to behave. The swimming pool downstairs came to mind and he wondered just how many laps he had done in the past six months in an effort to restrain himself. A hundred? More like five hundred.

Oh, well. He'd obtained his goal: Marissa was going to be his and that was all that mattered.

His hand slipped to her lap as he, too, drifted off to sleep, the most precious thing in his life held in his arms.

The next six days were a whirlwind of activity for Adam. He arranged for one of the judges to perform the ceremony Christmas morning in Marissa's apartment, something she insisted upon, saying his was too sterile for her taste. He'd arranged for flowers, a cake, a caterer to cook and serve the light lunch to his few guests, talked to her parents and made arrangements for them to fly in the day before. Finding a dressmaker to measure and fit Marissa for her dress on such short notice wasn't easy, but he finally located one, smoothing the way with greenbacks.

Marissa went along with whatever he said, her eyes dead, her voice flat. She agreed, but a part of her was gone—the part he loved the most. She was usually so sparkling, sharp-witted. So alive! He prayed she'd soon snap out of it, and then he prayed that she'd remain in this fog until the wedding was over so she wouldn't fight him at every turn.

When Christmas Eve came he knocked on her door, a brightly wrapped box that was almost as big as he was standing next to him. It was her wedding present—one he hoped she would love, and in loving it, understand how much he loved her.

Her eyes were wide when she opened the door, her expressive face glowing with curiosity for only a moment before resuming the passive look of the past week. Silently she moved aside and swung the door wider to allow him entrance.

"Merry Christmas," he murmured, brushing a kiss across her forehead because her head was lowered too far for him to touch her lips.

"Merry Christmas," she repeated.

The box had to be stood next to the tree, its large proportions not allowing it under the branches with the rest of the packages. Marissa watched as he maneuvered it into the corner. "Do I open that now or later?"

"Later. Do I fix myself a drink and would you like one?"

She smiled and the sadness of it nearly tore his heart out. "Wine's in the fridge and none for me, thank you."

Hands on his hips, he stared at her a moment. "Are you worried about tomorrow?"

"No."

"Pleased?"

"No."

"Scared?"

"Very much so."

"Why?"

"It's not every day a woman marries because the bundle of joy she's carrying needs a name. A father." Her voice was filled with that same trace of bitterness he had heard every day for six days.

"It happens more often than you know," Adam pointed out. "But that's not why we're marrying. We're doing this because I want you to be my wife."

"And the mother of your *legitimate* child."

He nodded. "That, too. But it's not the primary reason."

She turned away, walking toward the couch with her eyes down so she wouldn't have to see the look in his eyes. He studied her form, so round now that it was hard for her to stand or sit for long periods of time without the strain shadowing her eyes. She moved awkwardly, yet with the grace of her youth. Again stirrings shot through him. Again he wanted to groan with impatience.

He strode to her side, his hands resting on her shoulders as he stared down at her. Silence taunted him as she clamped her lips together. His fingers tightened, then stroked the silky fabric that covered her shoulders. She was wearing a dramatic-looking caftan of swirling, bright and dark colors. She was the most beautiful woman he had ever seen.

Without a word, his mouth swooped down to capture hers. Perhaps because he had taken her by surprise, Marissa's mouth opened willingly to his probing, her own tongue delicately caressing his as he sought the softness of her. With restrained care, he held her close, feeling her tummy against the hardness of him, sighing when her arms finally wound around his neck to embrace him. It was the first time since Thanksgiving that she had held him, and he wanted to cry with the beauty of it. Unknowingly he had been craving her touch, her embrace, her loving. He'd been drying up without it. But it was all right now—now he was filling with her love, exploding with the tenderness of her caring.

Adam pulled away reluctantly, holding her head against his chest as he stared at the ceiling and gave a small prayer of thanks for being able to hold Marissa again. Arms entwined, they stood clinging to each other. The Christmas-tree lights twinkled off and on, their moving patterns splashing the ceiling with pastel colors.

"Adam, I . . ."

"Shh," he whispered, his lips moving softly against her ear. "We're together and that's all that matters." He touched the dark curls that swirled around her shoulders. "Can you feel it, Marissa? The rightness of it? We *belong* together. Always."

She acquiesced, leaning against him. It was too peaceful a moment to shred with truths that had been uttered before.

Much later that night as Adam stretched out on the floor and sipped a brandy, Marissa tried to guess the contents of the large, gaily wrapped box by the side of the tree. Gone was her dour mood, replaced by the effervescence he'd missed so much. Her brown eyes twinkled with merriment as she popped one question after another.

"A camel?"

"No."

"An elephant?"

"Are you into animals?"

"A set of lawn furniture."

"No."

"I know. A set of microwave ovens."

"A set?

"Well—" she grinned, taking a breath and cradling her stomach with one hand, "—you have a tendency to overdo things."

His lips twitched as he tried to suppress a smile. "It's not a set of microwaves."

"Should I open it and end our misery?"

"I'm not miserable." His eyes warmed her insides.

She grabbed the ribbon and pulled. "And I'm not supposed to be miserable. After all, I'm in a delicate condition."

His brows rose as he eyed her rounded belly. "'Delicate'?"

She shot him a mock dirty look. "Delicate," she stated emphatically before turning back to the package and tearing off the paper. Opening the box was more difficult.

"Here," he said, standing and grabbing at the securely taped flap. "Now it's time for men's work."

She smiled as he snapped the tape. "The difference between brains and brawn? I agree."

He laughed aloud at her audacity, but when he looked at her, the laughter turned to hunger. Would he ever feel complete when she wasn't around him? He doubted it. He kissed the tip of her nose. "Merry

Christmas, soon-to-be Mrs. Pierce," he said, his voice husky with emotion.

"Merry Christmas," she said, her lips brushing over his, her brown eyes slumberous with the thoughts they shared.

He forced himself to turn away and flip open the box, knowing that anything they might want to do had to be postponed for a while.

Marissa peered in. "What is it?" Her eyes widened. "A dollhouse?"

He tore the box sides down until she could view the entire thing. "Yes. This one is for Taylor Jessica. The real one is about five miles from here and it's for Taylor's mom and dad."

Marissa stared from the house to Adam, then back again, her eyes wide. The house was huge, with a traditional two-story Georgian elevation at the front. But the back was all porched, making it look like a Southern plantation manor. The third-story gables had gingerbread trim. "'The real one'?" she repeated in amazement.

He watched her reaction, holding his breath. "I bought it at Thanksgiving. I picked the outside, you can do whatever it is you do to make it warm and cozy inside. Do you like it?"

Her head turned toward him slowly as if she were in a daze. "You bought it through Liz?"

He nodded, his heart dropping to his toes. It wasn't going to work. She didn't see his love in the gift. Liz was just the go-between. Nothing more.

Tears glazed her eyes and he yearned to hold her in his arms and tell her everything was going to be all right. But he couldn't take that chance. Her reaction would kill him.

"This was the real-estate deal you were working on?"

"Yes."

"Adam, I . . ." she began, then swallowed.

"You don't like it."

"I love it," she finally whispered, her hands cupping both sides of his face as she stared up at him. "I love you."

Silence hung in the air, waiting to be shattered, but he couldn't think of a thing to say. His breath stopped in his throat, his heart pounded so hard that he thought his head would explode. "Say it again." His voice was a growl. A plea. A demand.

She smiled and sunshine flooded his insides. "I love you. I love you so much, I hurt with happiness."

"My God," he sighed, pulling her into his arms and holding her as if he'd never let her go. "I've waited so long to hear you finally admit that."

"I did," she said, rubbing her face against the curve of his neck. "When my parents were here."

"No," he corrected. "They admitted it. You wouldn't say it even though I needed your words more than I needed anything in my whole life."

"I was scared."

"So was I."

She leaned her head back. "You? You've been a bully through this whole six months!"

"Because it was the only way I knew to hold you until you came to your senses and realized I was the only man in the world for you."

"Pompous."

"Stubborn."

"Arrogant."

"Darling."

She grinned. "I won't argue with that."

His chuckle reverberated through his chest as she snuggled close to him again. "You'd argue anything if you thought you could get a rise out of me."

"Is that what does it?" She nibbled on his neck. "I thought it was my fabulous shape and sexy walk."

"Marissa..." he began, and she stiffened in his arms. "What's wrong?"

She quickly smiled. "Nothing. When can we move?"

"Whenever you want."

"Next week?"

"Will you be up to it? After all, it will probably be your last week of pregnancy. You don't want to tire yourself out."

She chuckled. "No, *this* is my last week of pregnancy. I'm about to give you your Christmas present. Tonight."

He frowned, then his eyes grew wide. "Tonight?"

She nodded, a smile lighting her face. "They've been seven minutes apart until now."

He stood stock-still. "And now?"

She glanced at the clock on the mantel. "Five minutes apart."

From that moment on, everything was a blur. Adam did as he was told, finding her already packed suitcase, calling for the car to be brought around to the lobby doors, alerting the doctor and hospital that they were on their way. And through the storm of it all, Marissa walked calmly and with deliberation.

At one o'clock on Christmas morning Taylor Jessica Pierce was born. She weighed seven pounds, two ounces, and was nineteen inches long.

Her mother thought she was the spitting image of her father; her father thought she was perfect in every way.

At three o'clock on Christmas morning, while Marissa and Jessica slept, Adam Pierce prayed a thank-you message to God for giving him the one thing he had always craved, but had been afraid to label: a loving family of his own.

But just to ensure that his prayers were indeed answered, later that morning Adam had a justice of the peace hear the marriage vows in a crowded hospital room, with his new father-in-law, Garner, as best man, and Becca as maid of honor. After all, it took hard work and lots of luck to create a little magic.

And this was just the beginning. . . .

Take 4 best-selling love stories FREE
Plus get a FREE surprise gift!

Special Limited-Time Offer

Mail to   **Harlequin Reader Service**®

In the U.S.   In Canada
901 Fuhrmann Blvd.   P.O. Box 609
P.O. Box 1394   Fort Erie, Ontario
Buffalo, N.Y. 14240-1394   L2A 5X3

YES! Please send me 4 free Harlequin American
Romance® novels and my free surprise gift. Then send me 4
brand-new novels every month as they come off the presses. Bill
me at the low price of $2.49 each*—a 9% saving off the retail
price. There are no shipping, handling or other hidden costs.
There is no minimum number of books I must purchase. I can
always return a shipment and cancel at any time. Even if I never
buy another book from Harlequin, the 4 free novels and the
surprise gift are mine to keep forever.   154 BPA BP7F
*Plus 49¢ postage and handling per shipment in Canada.

Name _____ (PLEASE PRINT)

Address _____ Apt. No. _____

City _____ State/Prov. _____ Zip/Postal Code _____

This offer is limited to one order per household and not valid to present
subscribers. Price is subject to change.   AR-SUB-1B

ATTRACTIVE, SPACE SAVING BOOK RACK

Display your most prized novels on this handsome and sturdy book rack. The hand-rubbed walnut finish will blend into your library decor with quiet elegance, providing a practical organizer for your favorite hard-or soft-covered books.

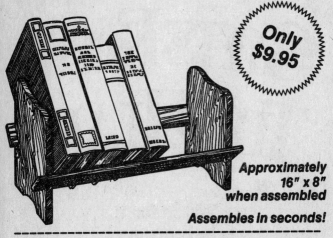

Only $9.95

Approximately 16" x 8" when assembled

Assembles in seconds!

To order, rush your name, address and zip code, along with a check or money order for $10.70* ($9.95 plus 75¢ postage and handling) payable to *Harlequin Reader Service*:

Harlequin Reader Service
Book Rack Offer
901 Fuhrmann Blvd.
P.O. Box 1396
Buffalo, NY 14269-1396

Offer not available in Canada.

BKR-1A

*New York and Iowa residents add appropriate sales tax.